Andrew Ma   ...en he was
seven and ha   ...at ne forgot to stop. He
has written ov   ...ty books, many of which have been
translated into foreign languages.

The idea for *Wolf Summer* came during a visit to the
UK Wolf Conservation Trust in Berkshire, when one
of the wolves rolled over on her back and invited
Andrew to scratch her stomach.

Andrew's interests include reading, listening to
music, history, photography and (of course) wolves.
He lives in Reading with his wife and their two cats.
The cats assist his writing by lying over his notebooks
and hiding pens under the sofa in the lounge.

with love for Jacky

and with thanks to the wolves and staff at
The UK Wolf Conservation Trust
Butlers Farm
Beenham
Berkshire
RG7 5NT

ORCHARD BOOKS
96 Leonard Street, London EC2A 4XD
Orchard Books Australia
Unit 31/56 O'Riordan Street, Alexandria, NSW 2015
First published in Great Britain in 2001
A PAPERBACK ORIGINAL
Text © Andrew Matthews 2001
The right of Andrew Matthews to be identified as the author
of this work has been asserted by him in accordance with
the Copyright, Designs and Patents Act, 1988.
A CIP catalogue record for this book is available
from the British Library.
ISBN 1 84121 758 1
3 5 7 9 10 8 6 4 2
Printed in Great Britain

wolfsummer

Andrew Matthews

ORCHARD BOOKS

1

Anna pressed her hand against Matt's chest and said, 'Time out.'

Matt frowned. 'What, now?'

'Definitely now.'

Matt's frown deepened into a scowl. He rolled on to his back and blinked at the ceiling.

'Sorry, Matt.'

'It's OK,' Matt said, not sounding OK.

'I'm afraid.'

'Of?'

'What might happen if we don't stop.'

'I know.'

'It's a compliment really.'

'You mean like I'm so horny it drives you wild.'

Very Matt: whenever romance threatened, he got basic.

'It's…bodies, isn't it?' said Anna.

'Huh?'

'Sex is bodies.'

'Bodies are nice,' Matt said with a grin.

'Yours is.'

'Not as nice as yours.'

Matt gently touched her; Anna quivered like a reflection on the surface of a pool.

'Don't, Matt!'

'Why not?'

'I like it too much.'

The sound of a lawnmower drifted in through the half-opened window. Anna noticed the way the light shone on Matt's skin.

'What are you thinking about, Matt?'

'Boiled cabbage.'

'Why boiled cabbage?'

'It helps calm me down. What are you thinking about?'

'You. Us.'

Us was still new enough for Anna not to be used to it. She'd written *Anna and Matt* all over her English coursework folder to try and convince herself that it was real. For months she'd worried that she'd never have a boyfriend, and now there was Matt – the first person who'd cared for her without having to.

'Matt, what d'you like best about me?'

Matt took a moment to consider. 'Your eyes. What d'you like best about me?'

'The way you make me feel.'

Matt wiggled his eyebrows. 'Hmm!'

'No, not like that! Even just walking down the street with you, I—'

Car tyres scrunched on the gravel of the driveway; Anna sat up.

'What?' said Matt.

A car engine stopped; a handbrake made a noise like a marimba.

Anna said, 'Oh my God, it's Dad. He's early!'

In a slow-motion film, Matt twisted around and started to haul on his jeans; Anna fumbled with the armholes of her top.

A key rattled in the front-door lock.

'Quick, hide in the bathroom!' Anna hissed.

It was already too late.

'Anna?' Dad called. 'Anna?'

Matt mouthed, 'Don't say anything!' but Anna knew that it wouldn't work.

'I'm in my bedroom, Dad.'

Footsteps climbed the stairs, approached along the landing.

Matt's face was white and his eyes were blank.

Dad said, 'What are you doing indoors on a day like this?'

The bedroom door bumped against the drawn bolt.

'Anna, why have you locked the door?'

'You can't come in, Dad.'

'Why ever not?'

The film speeded up. In her imagination, Anna saw a silent-movie comedy in which Matt clambered through the window and down the drainpipe. She was out of time and excuses; with a calmness that surprised her, Anna said, 'Matt's with me. We haven't got all our clothes on.'

There was a long pause before Dad said, 'Get dressed, the pair of you. I'll wait downstairs.'

Anna clung to Matt, holding him as tightly as she could.

Matt said, 'What's going to happen, Anna? What will he do?'

'I don't know,' said Anna.

*

Dad was seated on the sofa in the lounge. Anna had thought he'd be furious, but he seemed more tired than anything.

'This is my fault,' Dad said quietly. 'I thought I could trust you two alone together. I thought you were mature enough to—' He sighed.

'I'm sorry, Mr Cope,' said Matt.

'So am I, Matthew. I think you should leave.'

Matt ran his hand through his hair. 'Mr Cope, if I promise not to do anything like this again, can I still see Anna?'

'That wouldn't be appropriate, Matthew. It would be far better for all concerned if you kept away from my daughter in future. Is that clear?'

'Yes.'

Hot tears coursed down Anna's cheeks. She wiped them away and said, 'Can I go to the door with Matt to say goodbye?'

Dad nodded. 'Make it brief.'

Out in the hallway, Anna kissed Matt fiercely.

'It isn't over!' she whispered. 'We'll find a way!'

'I know we will,' said Matt. He opened the front door and walked down the drive. When he reached the street he broke into a run.

*

The worst part was the questions. It would have been better if Dad had shouted, but instead he turned into Dr Cope and adopted his best clinical manner.

'How long have you and Matthew had a physical relationship?'

Impossible question: from the first moment they laid eyes on each other; since the first kiss?

'I don't know,' Anna said.

'Did he force himself on you?'

'Of course not!'

'So you were a willing partner?'

'Yes.'

'Did you have penetrative sex?'

Anna's face burned with humiliation; all her privacy was gone.

'Do you know what that means, Anna?'

'Yes, and no we didn't.'

'You're quite sure?'

'Yes.'

Dad looked relieved. 'Well that's something to be thankful for, I suppose. What were you thinking of, Anna?'

'Nothing. I didn't think.'

'That much is obvious. Couldn't you have restrained yourself, exercised some self-control?'

'We weren't doing anything wrong!'

'Nonsense! You knew very well that what you were doing was wrong. You and Matthew are both under age. You're an intelligent girl, Anna – how could you be so irresponsible? Good God, if you're like this at fifteen!'

'Tell my body, Dad!'

'*What?*'

'Tell my body fifteen's not old enough!' Anna knew that she was making things worse, but she couldn't hold back. 'When did you start – or did sex come out of nowhere on your sixteenth birthday?'

Dad reached flashpoint. 'That's enough, Anna!' he snapped. 'Go to your room. We'll discuss this later when your mother comes home.'

Anna hadn't been ordered to her room since she was eight; if the circumstances hadn't been so awful, it would have been ludicrous.

By the time Mum arrived home from work, Anna was all out of defiance. She dreaded talking to Mum: when faced with a crisis, Dad became stuffy and aggressive; Mum tended to under-react and remained calm, almost serene. She could lay a guilt trip better than anyone else Anna knew.

Anna lay curled up on her bed, listening to her parents' voices rise through the floorboards. She couldn't make out any words, but their tones were unmistakable – Dad's sharp, Mum's soothing and reasonable.

A few moments after the talking stopped, Mum tapped on Anna's door.

'Anna, can I come in?'

'Yes.'

Mum entered the room and sat on the edge of the bed. She reached out and brushed back a lock of hair that was stuck to Anna's forehead.

'We weren't doing anything bad, Mum!' Anna blurted. 'We were only making out.'

Making out sounded pathetic when she said it to Mum.

Mum smiled sorrowfully.

'Your father's disappointed in you,' she said. 'He feels that you've let him down.'

'Why – because I'm sexually active? I'm not perfect, Mum.'

'You were in his eyes. Finding you with Matt gave him a shock.'

'I'm sorry.'

'Sorry for what you did or sorry that you were caught?'

Anna couldn't think of an answer.

Mum said, 'He wants to send you to a boarding school, so you and Matt won't see each other in September.'

'He can't do that!'

'Don't worry, I'll talk him out of it, but we still have a problem.'

'Oh?'

'You've lost his trust, Anna. He doesn't feel you can be left alone during the day.'

'What's he going to do, stay off work so he can follow me everywhere?'

Mum sighed.

'Sarcasm won't help, Anna. You've hurt him badly and he needs time to heal. I think it would be a good idea for you both to be apart for a while, let the air clear and get things into perspective. My suggestion is that you spend the rest of the summer with your grandmother.'

'But she lives in the back of beyond!'

'Exactly.'

Anna knew Gran had moved recently, but she hadn't seen the new house. She remembered where Gran used to live, the cramped terraced house where every window looked out on brick walls and the tiny kitchen was only big enough for one. She didn't want to spend the whole summer in a place like that.

'Gran won't want me there!' Anna protested. 'You can't dump me on her just like that.'

'No one's dumping anyone,' Mum said, 'and Gran will be delighted. I'll tell your father that you thought of it and get him to ring her.'

'Does she have to know about...?'

'I think it's only fair, don't you?'

'It would make a difference if I said no?' Anna said sarcastically.

'Anna, please try and understand. Your father's a doctor. He's treated dozens of pregnant teenage girls. He's seen the damage that underage sex can do and he's afraid for you.'

'And how about you, Mum?'

Mum paused, then said, 'What matters most is that you realise that what you did wasn't right. Until you admit that to yourself, my opinion is irrelevant.'

2

When Anna woke up in the morning, the misery was still there. She cried quietly into her pillow, whispering Matt's name over and over as though it would bring him back. When she couldn't cry any more she lay still, listening to her parents moving about downstairs. She felt hollow inside, like the ruins of a bombed-out city. The bright sunshine seeping in around the edges of the drawn curtains mocked her.

'It ought to be grey and raining,' she thought.

There was nothing to look forward to, no one she wanted to see; except Matt.

Anna waited until she heard Dad's car drive off, then got out of bed and went downstairs. Mum was in the kitchen, loading breakfast plates into the dishwasher. She gave Anna a sad-eyed smile and said, 'Did you sleep all right?'

'Not really,' Anna said. 'How's Dad?'

'Stern and silent. What are you going to do this morning?'

'I don't know.'

'You should sort out what clothes you're going to take to Gran's. I can give you a hand. I'm going to work at home today.'

'Keeping tabs on me in case I sneak off to meet Matt?' Anna said bitterly. 'What if he comes here?'

'I'll ask him to leave,' said Mum. She stepped over to Anna and hugged her. 'I know it's awful now, but things will get better.'

'Will they?' said Anna, thinking that things would never be better again.

'Of course they will.' Mum let Anna go and tried to sound bright. 'Is Maggie back from France yet?'

'Yes.'

'Why don't you give her a call and invite her over? We could all go out to lunch somewhere.'

Anna wasn't certain about lunch, but talking to Maggie seemed like a really good idea.

*

Maggie turned up looking gorgeous and knowing it, wearing a short-sleeved white T-shirt to show off her French tan. Mum greeted her with more than a little relief, then went into the garden to do paperwork, leaving the two girls in the lounge.

Maggie listened to Anna's tale of woe, pulled sympathetic faces and said, 'Oh, God!' in the appropriate places. After the tale was finished, she said, 'So what happens now?'

'I go to Gran's tomorrow. I won't be back until the weekend before term starts,' said Anna.

'And Matt?'

'We're not supposed to have any contact.'

'That's going to be difficult come September, isn't it? You're in the same English and History sets as Matt.'

Anna shrugged. 'I haven't thought that far ahead. Maybe by then, Dad will have calmed down enough to let me and Matt get back together.'

'If you still want to,' said Maggie.

'Meaning?'

'You guys have been an item since Easter. That's practically a record in our year. Most people get bored with each other after six weeks or so.'

'Are you saying that Matt's bored with me?'

'No, but…' Maggie sighed. 'Be realistic, Anna. Plenty of girls have got the hots for Matt, and with you out of the way, they'll be tempted to make a move. Matt wasn't exactly Mr Faithful before he went out with you. Out of sight, out of mind – you know?'

'And absence makes the heart grow fonder. Thanks for the vote of confidence, Maggie!'

'I just don't want to see my best mate eating her heart out over someone who isn't worth it.'

'You don't think Matt's worth it?'

Maggie had dug herself into a hole, couldn't find a way out and decided to dig a little deeper. 'You could do better. Matt's a bit of a smoothie, isn't he?'

'That was before!' Anna said hotly. 'He's different with me. You don't know him the way I do.'

Maggie sensed a squabble brewing and made a tactical withdrawal. 'Anything I can do to help?' she said.

'Yes – talk to him for me. Tell him I'm not going to stop feeling how I feel about him. He's as upset as I am. Be a shoulder for him, will you, Maggie? Let me know how he's doing.'

'You've got it. I'll watch him like a hawk and call

you as soon as anything happens.'

'No, no phone calls. Gran might listen in. Write to me.'

Maggie looked shocked. '*Write* to you – as in snail mail? Isn't your Gran on the net?'

'She doesn't have a computer.'

'No computer? How does she manage?'

'Guess I'm about to find out,' Anna said.

3

It was difficult to write. The train kept swaying, making Anna's handwriting go all over the place, but she stuck at it. The headphones of the mini-disc player kept the world at arm's length. The music provided an odd soundtrack to the comings and goings of the other passengers – guys in grey suits sipped coffee from plastic beakers to a techno beat – and saved her from the loud voices of people using their mobiles.

I'm writing this for you, Matt. You'll get to read it some time, but not for a while yet because they made me promise not to phone you or send you any letters or e-mails. I'm going to keep the promise, to show them that they're wrong. They think that if we don't have any contact our feelings for each other will change, but I know that what we've got won't ever change. It isn't just a crush, it's REAL and we're going to prove it.

I'm on a train. They're sending me to my gran's for the summer – like out of sight, out of mind? They don't want us to bump into each other by accident – or on purpose. On the way to the station, my dad said, 'You'll thank us for this one day, Anna.'

Can you believe that?

Missing you goes right through me. It starts the minute I wake up and it doesn't stop when I go to sleep, because I dream about you. I like the dreams better than the waking up part.

I wish I could hold you. I need that 'just us' feeling. Before I left, I made a recording of our favourite tracks. Right now I'm listening to that song that was playing the first time we danced together at the Easter disco – remember? I never realised before, but it's a sad song about breaking up. All the songs I recorded sound sad. It's hard when the only person who can help is the one person you're not allowed to see.

Where are you? Are you as miserable as I am? I used to be able to tell when you were thinking about me, because I could feel you in my head. I've lost that feeling. You're too far away.

Why can't time speed up so I can be old enough to live

my own life instead of having my parents on my back, controlling everything I do and everywhere I go? They want me to feel guilty about us, but I don't. They're the guilty ones. They can't handle it that I'm not their best little girl any more. Seeing me reminds them of how unfair they're being, so they've dumped me on Gran to get me out of the way. They talk like sex is something dirty and wrong. Something must have happened for them to think like that. They're warped.

Writing things down is a bit like talking to you, but only a bit. You can't touch thoughts. Thoughts don't squeeze your hand and tell you things are going to be all right. They will be all right, won't they, Matt?

They have to be.

Gran was waiting on the platform when Anna stepped off the train. She was tall and slender with dyed brown hair cut short like a man's; apart from that, there was nothing masculine about Gran. She had her own sense of style: battered black leather jacket, stone-washed denim jeans and white trainers with yellow sparkly laces. The outfit suited her. She didn't look anywhere near sixty-five.

Gran gave Anna a loose-elbowed wave, then rushed

over and hugged her. Anna kept herself stiff, to show that she'd rather be someplace else.

Gran said, 'Look at you! You make me feel like a little old lady.'

'Why?'

'You're so grown-up.'

'Not according to Mum and Dad.'

A doubtful expression crossed Gran's face; evidently she wasn't quite ready to go into the reasons behind Anna's visit.

'How was your journey?'

'Boring.'

'I left the car in the station car-park. I thought we'd lock your case in the boot, grab a bite somewhere and have a look round the shops. How does that sound?'

It sounded like shopping therapy and all-girls-together. Anna could see what was coming: Gran would try and gain her confidence to soften her up, then lay down the law. Gran had probably worked out the plan in advance with Mum and Dad.

Mum, Dad and Gran: an unbeatable combination.

Anna and Gran had lunch in the town centre. A room in the old Town Hall had been converted into a bar-cum-buffet. From her seat by the window, Anna could see a statue of Queen Victoria on a plinth outside. Queen Victoria had a sceptre in her right hand and an orb in her left. It reminded Anna of the joke Gran used to tell about the statue – *Queen Victoria will be holding a ball in Town Hall Square tonight.*

Gran chatted about people she knew, names that Anna couldn't put a face to. She described her trip to Monet's garden in France; a local art shop wanted to mount a small exhibition of her paintings; someone had commissioned her to do a portrait of the family cat.

'You sound busy,' said Anna.

'I like to keep busy. If I stand still I might rust.'

'Won't I be in the way?'

'Not if you keep out of it. I hope you're not expecting me to wait on you hand and foot. You'll have to tidy your own room and do your fair share of the cooking. And I don't iron.'

'Excuse me?'

'I gave up ironing when I retired from teaching. Ironing is the pits!'

In spite of herself, Anna smiled.

Gran frowned. 'You're not eating.'

'I'm not hungry.'

'You must eat, Anna, or you'll make yourself ill.'

To avoid being nagged, Anna chewed on a piece of endive.

'Anna, I know you're depressed,' Gran said cautiously. 'Believe it or not, I was your age once and I know how it feels.'

Here we go! Anna thought.

'I expect you consider your stay as a punishment.'

'Isn't it?'

'Not as far as I'm concerned. I'm pleased to see you. I've got my fingers crossed that some of your youth is going to rub off on me – and I'm dying to show you the new house.' Gran leaned closer across the table and lowered her voice. 'I know you're having problems, Anna. I want to make it clear that they're your problems and you're the one who has to deal with them. If you want to talk about them I'll listen, and if you don't want to talk about them I'll listen to you being quiet. What I won't do is interfere or take sides. D'you see what I'm getting at?'

'I think so.'

'I'll give you advice if you ask for it, as long as you do the same for me.'

'Sorry?'

Just for a second, Gran's eyes went off somewhere else. 'Even at my age you can still get yourself into messes. The only difference between being sixty and sixteen is that you don't have to live so long with your mistakes.'

Anna felt uneasy. Gran was hinting that there was more to her life than being an ex-teacher with an interest in art. What could it be? Anna had always figured that old people were used up; they'd had their portion of what was on offer and the only problems they had were physical ones, like arthritis. She'd thought of Gran as Gran: a slightly eccentric, unbelievably well-organised, independent lady who turned Dad into a little boy whenever he was around her. Now she began to suspect that there might be someone else in Gran, an actual person that Anna didn't know anything about.

They hit the shops. Gran picked out clothes for Anna that Anna wouldn't have picked herself – shiny metallic-looking short skirts, tops with patterns like migraine attacks. She insisted that Anna try them on and Anna went along with it. The clothes were too expensive to buy, and Anna wouldn't have wanted them anyway. She got the idea that Gran was getting her to experiment with her appearance, find a new look for a new Anna.

Gran took Anna to the cosmetics department of a big store, saying that she needed Anna's help choosing a lipstick. She tested the samples on the back of her hand until it was covered with different coloured stripes, like a Native American's warpaint.

'How about *Scarlet Surrender*? Do you think I'm a *Scarlet Surrender* person, Anna?'

'Uh-uh. Too tarty. The browny one's better.'

'What, *Maraschino Autumn*? You could be right. What colour lipstick do you use?'

'I don't.'

Gran cocked an eyebrow. 'Every little helps, my dear. Flaunt it while you've got it – it's a long time gone.'

As Gran was paying for the lipstick, Anna said, 'I like your new hairdo, Gran. You've gone a different colour from the last time I saw you.'

'It was bright orange the last time you saw me. Tragic mistake. I've been thinking about owning up and letting it grow out white.'

'Don't. You'd look like a younger woman with old hair.'

Gran laughed. 'Keep on saying things like that and

you can stay as long as you want.'

I'm nearly having fun! Anna thought. I shouldn't be. I'm grieving for Matt.

Gran caught the look in Anna's eyes and nudged her with an elbow. 'Men, huh? Can't live with them, can't live without them.'

'Ain't that the truth, Gran.'

On the way out of town, they got snarled up in traffic. Gran's pessimistic streak showed. 'This is characteristic of the pattern of movement around a road accident,' she said darkly.

Anna wondered how you could tell stuff like that; a line of slow-moving cars was just a line of slow-moving cars.

'I actually used to enjoy driving,' said Gran. 'It gave me a sense of freedom. Funny how when you put a lot of free people together, they form a gridlock.'

Gran was wrong, there was no sign of any accident, but it still took ages to get through the jam and by the time they were out in the country the sun was setting.

'I hope you're going to like the house,' Gran said. 'It's a converted barn.'

'You wrote and told us about it. You didn't send any pictures, though.'

'I wanted people to come and see it for themselves, but nobody took the hint. I've made a splendid job of the garden, if I do say so myself.'

After fifteen minutes of sunset fields and black clumps of woodland, Gran turned off the road and made a sharp left into a bumpy lane. She stopped the car; Anna got out and looked around.

If Gran hadn't told her, Anna wouldn't have known that the house had once been a barn. The front garden was as impressive as Gran had claimed: a rockery with alpine plants; ornamental grasses in a bed of gravel. It felt peaceful. Overhead the moon was up, blue and half full in a sky where the first stars showed as pale dots.

Gran opened the front door, turned on a light and stood on the threshold, her arms spread in a gesture of welcome.

There was a sound from far off: a warbling howl that yearned upwards and dropped sharply down. Another howl joined it, and another, and another.

The hairs on Anna's arms prickled and she shuddered. 'What's that, Gran?'

Gran smiled broadly. 'That's the wolves,' she said.

4

There are wolves *here, Matt! I heard them earlier on when I arrived at Gran's place. Gran was – oh yeah, wolves, no big deal. It was totally unreal. They're going to give me nightmares.*

Gran told me about the wolves over dinner. This bunch of people have set up a wolf sanctuary on a farm near the house. (Bet they're a bunch of tree-hugging hippies.) They want to overcome the public's prejudice about wolves, or something. Like just because wolves attack and eat people, they can't be all bad.

I asked Gran if she was frightened of living so close to dangerous animals. Not Gran! Turns out she knows one of the guys who runs the sanctuary. They used to teach together years ago. Gran helps out at the sanctuary once a week, clearing up wolf poo and stuff. Mm, n-i-i-c-e!

I'm nervous. What if the wolves break out and surround the house?

I've never heard wolves howling live before. It's weird, kind of terrifying and sad at the same time. They sound like they're calling because they're lonely. I know how that *feels.*

I love this house. It's a converted barn – not as bad as it sounds. When you step in the front door, you're in the kitchen. Then you go down some steps into this huge space with an upstairs balcony-thing that goes right round three walls. It's a dining room and lounge in one. Gran's put up loads of shelves for her books, and there are two sofas, two armchairs, a piano and a dining table and chairs. The floor's made of pine blocks. Gran's spread rugs all over it instead of having a carpet. Off the big room is a conservatory that Gran uses as a studio – I told you she paints, didn't I? Some of her stuff isn't bad. It looks like what it's supposed to be.

My bedroom's at the top of the stairs. That's where I'm writing this. You're here too. I've got one of the photos we had taken in that booth. I put it in a little frame, and it's on my bedside table. When I look at the photo and see how happy I am, I think I can't be the same person as I was then.

Does hurt change things, Matt? Like after you've been hurt, can you go back to the same as you were before? I hope so. I don't want either of us to change. But suppose we do? Suppose one of us changes more than the other?

I guess there are more frightening things than wolves around. People, for instance.

Anna didn't get up until gone nine. She found Gran out on the patio, reading the morning mail. Breakfast things were set out on a garden table. In the centre of the table was a bowl of fruit.

'There's tea in the pot,' said Gran. 'If you want anything else you can get it yourself.'

'Just tea is fine.'

'Help yourself to fruit.'

It was closer to a command than an invitation. Anna took a satsuma from the bowl and began to peel it.

The patio looked out over the back garden. Beyond the end of the garden was a view of a narrow valley surrounded by low, wooded hills. The warm sunshine made the countryside seem more like Italy than Berkshire.

'It's going to be hot, according to the forecast,' said

Gran. 'I have to do some work on that cat painting this morning. You should get some sunbathing in.'

'I didn't bring a swimming cozzie.'

'Sunbathe in your undies. Nobody will see you, it's very private here. You'll find suntan lotion in the bathroom cabinet. I thought we might go for a walk this afternoon.'

'Where?'

'Just around, so you can get your bearings.'

Anna ate the satsuma. The only sound was the breeze in the leaves of the cherry tree at the edge of the lawn.

'Don't you get fed up living here on your own, Gran?' Anna asked. 'It's so quiet.'

'After a career teaching in secondary schools, quiet comes as a blessed relief, believe you me.'

'D'you ever miss Grandad?'

'No.'

'Are you in touch with him?'

Gran peered over the top of her reading spectacles. 'Why would I want to be – and why would he, for that matter? We were married for twenty years. We said everything we had to say to each other then. Are you in touch with him?'

Grandad lived in America; Anna had never met him.

'Kind of,' she said. 'We get a card from him every Christmas. We don't send him one though, and Dad never says anything about him.'

'He wouldn't.'

'Why's that?'

Gran took off her spectacles and placed them on the table. 'The divorce came as a shock to your father. He never forgave John for what he did.'

'John?'

'Your grandfather.'

'What did he do?'

'Nothing remarkable. He met a younger woman, fell in love and left me for her.'

'How did you—I mean—' Anna faltered. 'Sorry, Gran. Are you OK with talking about this?'

'Perfectly. It's all water under the bridge.'

'When Grandad left you, how did you feel?'

'Used. Betrayed. Jealous. Angry.'

'Because you still loved him?'

Gran shrugged. 'I don't know.'

Anna frowned: how could you not know if you were in love?

'Then why did you marry him in the first place?' she said.

'We had to get married. I was pregnant, and in those days men who made young women pregnant did the honourable thing.'

'So you weren't in love with each other?'

'We were both very much in love at the start.'

'What went wrong?'

'Nothing. At some point we fell out of love without realising. There were more and more rows, less and less kissing and making up. I was so unhappy and stressed, I had a nervous breakdown. I was a voluntary patient in a psychiatric ward for three months. That's where I took up painting. Art lessons were part of my therapy.'

Anna couldn't think what to say.

Gran chuckled. 'I did get over it, you know. I've got a signed certificate that says I'm sane. You won't meet many people with one of those.'

'How can you fall out of love, Gran? I thought true love was supposed to last for ever.'

'People only live happily ever after in fairy tales, I'm afraid. Real life is a lot tougher. You can fall out of love as easily as you can fall into it. Living with someone day in and day out isn't easy. We all have little habits that others find extremely irritating.'

'What was Grandad's most irritating habit?'

'The way he stirred his tea. He always tapped his spoon three times on the rim of the cup.'

'And that made you stop loving him?'

'That and his stubbornness, and his refusal to admit that he was ever in the wrong.'

'Like Dad.'

'Exactly like your father. That's why they don't get on.'

Anna's stomach gurgled like a blocked drain.

'I'd feed that ravenous beast if I were you,' said Gran. 'Go and make yourself some toast.' She put her spectacles back on and opened an envelope.

As Anna stood up, a thought struck her. 'Gran, have you been in love with anyone since you got divorced?'

Without looking at Anna, Gran said, 'I refuse to answer that question, on the grounds that I might incriminate myself.'

Anna took it as a yes.

After lunch, just when Anna and Gran were about to set off on their walk, Gran had a visitor. A dilapidated pick-up truck bounced up the lane and pulled in beside Gran's car. A man got out of the truck, holding a cardboard carton. He was medium height but looked taller because of the way he held his shoulders straight. He had swept-back white hair, a white beard, bristling eyebrows and a nose like an eagle's beak. Anna thought he looked like an Ancient Greek god.

'I was just passing. I thought you might like some eggs,' the man said to Gran.

'I have plenty, thanks.'

The man grunted and thrust the carton into Gran's hands. 'Just take the bloody eggs will you, woman! I've never known anyone like you for looking a gift-horse in the mouth.' He glanced at Anna. 'Who is this stunning young lady?'

'My granddaughter, Anna. Anna, this is Zack.'

Zack gave Anna's hand a warm, firm shake.

'Pleased to meet you, Anna,' he said. 'Are you down here on holiday?'

'Um, yes.'

'And you chose to spend it with this mad old bat? Rather you than me!'

'I'd rather be mad than an obsessive,' Gran said tartly.

'Who's an obsessive?'

'You are.'

'I am not an obsessive. I'm dedicated.'

'Zack's the old colleague I was telling you about last night,' Gran explained to Anna.

'What, the wolf man?'

Zack threw back his head and laughed. 'Don't worry, you're quite safe. It's not a full moon tonight, so I shan't sprout fur and fangs.'

'Pity, it might be an improvement,' said Gran.

Zack laughed again. 'That's what I like – a duel of wits with an unarmed opponent. Well, since it's obvious that no one is going to offer me the courtesy of a cup of tea, I'll be on my way. See you on Thursday, Joanna.'

'You'll have that privilege and pleasure, yes,' said Gran.

'Bring Anna along, if she wants to.'

Gran and Anna watched Zack drive off. Gran waved just before the pick-up turned out of sight.

Anna said, 'Zack's amazing-looking, isn't he?'

'Is he? I've known him so long that I've stopped noticing his looks.'

'Are you two always like that?'

'Like what?'

'Insulting each other all the time.'

'You have to insult Zack or he's inclined to take over. I've found that it pays to keep him on a short leash.'

'But you're good friends really?'

'More like old sparring partners. Zack can be charming company, but most of the time he's impossible.'

Something in Gran's voice made Anna turn to look at her. Gran's face was wearing a wistful, puzzled expression. Anna wondered what had put it there.

5

I don't know what's happening to me, and I'm worried. I keep having these panic attacks where—

OK, OK. If you were here, you'd tell me to calm down and take it from the top. So, calm, yeah?

I've been doing all right so far. Ish. But yesterday wasn't all right. I went for a walk with Gran in the afternoon. It was stinking hot, the kind of heat that feels like a headache, you know? We were in the country – like where else is there to be round here? Anyway, we crossed this field with these horses in it, and one of them came over, on the scrounge. He let me stroke his muzzle and pat his neck. Did I ever tell you I was mad on horses when I was a kid? I watched every TV programme going on horses. I nagged Mum and Dad into paying for me to have riding lessons. It took them eighteen months to cave in. I had this big fantasy about riding for Britain in the Olympic Games, and a little fantasy that I was a natural rider – like as soon as I sat on a horse's back I'd know what to do without being taught.

How wrong was I? I was a total klutz. I kept falling off. After I dislocated my shoulder, Dad put his foot down and said I couldn't go to lessons any more. I sulked, but I didn't mind that much, because by that time I'd started getting interested in boys. All the pictures of ponies that I'd put on my bedroom wall came down, and posters of boy bands went up.

Guess I would have been better off sticking with horses.

At the far side of the field Gran and I crossed a concrete bridge that went over a ditch. The ditch was dry and at the bottom was a grass snake sunning itself on a stone. First time I've ever seen one. Half of me was – ARGH, A SNAKE! – the other half was fascinated, like when you see something that's disgusting but you can't stop staring at it? The snake was incredibly green. If it had moved, I would have been out of there right away, but it looked like a necklace lying there on the stone.

Now comes the worrying part. Gran wanted to show me this pool where she'd seen kingfishers. We were strolling down a lane, and I got this crazy idea that if I thought about you hard enough, I could make you be there.

And I couldn't remember what colour your eyes are. I know they're grey, but I couldn't remember the exact shade. All I could think of was the photo in my bedroom, and that's too small to show your eyes properly.

What does it mean, Matt? It's only just over a week since I saw you, and you're already starting to fade. Is it the same for you? Am I fading when you think about me? That's why I'm worried. Does love only work when two people are plugged into it? Does it stop if they get disconnected?

At least here I don't have to go places we've been together, which makes things easier, but I'm apart from everything, so I don't know what's going on. I wish Maggie would hurry up and get in touch, like she said she would. She promised to let me know how you are. I just hope that no news is good news.

I'm numb, frozen over inside. In some places the ice is thin and my feet go through into mud that I can't wash off.

I need you to thaw me. I want to feel things again, instead of being a frozen mess.

*

On Wednesday evening Anna tried to watch TV with Gran, but she couldn't concentrate. Her mind kept going back to the moment when things had gone wrong: the sound of Dad climbing the stairs; the look on Matt's face. She was trapped in a loop of 'ifs' – if she and Matt had gone ice-skating like they'd arranged to, if she hadn't insisted on going upstairs, if Dad had come home at his usual time – it would have been so easy for things to be different.

Anna stirred in her chair. 'I'm going to make myself a hot chocolate, Gran. Would you like one?'

'No thanks.'

Anna wasn't fussed about the hot chocolate, but she had to do something to break her chain of thought, before she had a screaming fit. She went up the steps to the kitchen and filled the kettle.

Gran switched off the TV. 'Walls starting to close in on you?'

'Kind of.'

'You must be missing your friends.'

Anna wondered if Gran meant Matt. 'Yeah, I am.'

'What would you normally be doing now?'

'Not a lot. Hanging out. How about you?'

'Me?'

'What do you normally do on Wednesday night?'

'What I'm doing now, except that I'd be talking to myself instead of you.'

'Not meeting up with friends?'

'Oh yes! My life's a frantic social whirl. Having you around is cramping my style.'

The kettle boiled. Anna spooned powdered chocolate into a mug, poured in hot water and stirred carefully. 'Is it really cramping your style?' she asked.

'No,' said Gran. 'Most of my friends are married. That can be a little awkward.'

'Why?'

'Because I'm single. I catch them feeling sorry for me. Occasionally they try to pair me off with an unattached male. Most embarrassing.'

'Is Zack married?'

'He's a widower. Now he's married to his precious wolves. Just as well, he'd never find a woman who'd put up with him.' Gran pulled a face. 'Do you intend to stir the bottom out of that mug?'

'Sorry.'

Anna went back into the front room, sat on the sofa and tucked her legs up under her.

'Is that comfort food?' said Gran.

'Uh-huh. When all else fails, try chocolate.'

'Or fruit cake, in my case. Nothing like glacé cherries for chasing the blues away.'

'What do you get the blues about?'

'This and that. Look, Anna, if you're coming down with cabin fever, why don't you come with me to the wolf sanctuary tomorrow?'

'I'm not so sure that would be a good idea. I have a thing about dogs. Anything bigger than a spaniel brings me out in a cold sweat.'

'What are you afraid of?'

'Er, getting my throat ripped out.'

'Dogs are aggressive if they've been trained to be, or if they've been abused. Wolves are different.'

'How?'

'Come with me tomorrow and find out.'

It was looking increasingly as if Anna didn't have a choice. 'Can I stay in the car?' she said nervously.

'You'll be perfectly safe as long as you remember the rules. Don't wear loose jackets or anything with dangly bits, no leather or suede coats, no strong perfume—'

'Perfume?'

'It gets the wolves over-excited.'

Anna shuddered at the thought of an over-excited wolf. 'I don't know, Gran.'

'Do you think I'd take you if there were any risk of your being hurt?'

'No, but...'

Anna paused: what was that *but*?

But was a thousand fairy stories about princesses being chased through forests, old horror movies with eyes glowing in the dark. Wolves were savage killers and once they were on your trail they didn't quit. Wolves were wild and the idea of getting close to an animal that was out of control terrified Anna. She quickly changed the subject.

'Gran, what colour are Grandad's eyes?'

Gran did a double take. 'What prompted that question?'

'Just curious.'

'Blue, like yours and your father's.'

'Does Dad look like him?'

'Not as much as you do.'

'I do?' Anna was genuinely curious now. 'I didn't know that. I haven't even seen a picture of him.'

'I can't oblige you there, I'm afraid. When the divorce papers came through, I took all my old photographs and letters and burned them at the bottom of the garden.'

'Why did you do that?'

'Because it was healthier than keeping them. When something is over, you have to let it go.'

'And it was that easy – one bonfire and that was it?'

'No, but it was a start. You should get rid of pain as quickly as you can, whether it's physical or emotional. Suffering doesn't make people noble, it twists them.'

Anna disagreed. The pain she felt for Matt was a test of how much she loved him; she was going to pass the test, because love always won in the end.

The phone rang at nine. Gran answered, and it was obvious that Mum or Dad was on the other end of the line.

Gran said, 'Why don't you ask her yourself?' and held the phone out to Anna. 'It's your father.'

Anna didn't budge.

'You have to talk to him at some point,' said Gran. 'You may as well do it now and get it over with.'

Reluctantly, Anna stood up, crossed the room and took the phone. 'Hello,' she said.

'Hello, Anna,' said Dad. 'How are you?' He sounded

as though he were talking to one of his patients.

'OK.'

'Are you getting on all right with your grandmother?'

'Yes.'

'What have you been doing?'

'Nothing. Walking. Talking.'

'Talking about what?'

'Stuff.'

Dad sighed. 'It's quiet here without you. Your mother and I miss you.'

Anna almost laughed. It was *so* Dad. He couldn't come right out and say, *I miss you*, he had to include Mum as well.

'Really?' she said. 'I hope you're not expecting any sympathy.'

It came out harder than she'd intended.

Dad's voice went cold. 'Let's not pick an argument, Anna. Put your grandmother on, would you?'

Anna handed the phone back to Gran and went to slouch on the sofa. She couldn't do anything right; when she talked to Dad, it all came out wrong. Were they going to be that awkward with each other for the rest of their lives?

Gran finished the conversation and replaced the

receiver on its cradle. 'It's early days, Anna,' she said.

Anna was so wrapped up in herself that she didn't notice how Gran had read her mind.

'What is it with him?' she grumbled. 'Why can't he say what he means?'

'He's a man,' Gran said. 'The vast majority of males consider expressing their emotions as a sign of weakness.'

'Why?'

Gran smiled. 'Because they're afraid,' she said.

6

Anna staggered downstairs at seven thirty. Gran was already up, poaching eggs in the kitchen; she was dressed in dark blue dungarees.

'Did you sleep well?' Gran asked.

'I'll tell you when I'm awake,' said Anna. 'I'd forgotten that this time of the morning existed.'

'Pour the tea, would you? I'll serve the eggs.'

Anna's stomach turned over. 'I think I'll just have toast.'

But Gran was having no nonsense. 'You need a proper breakfast – it's the most important meal of the day.'

Once Anna had forced down the first mouthful, she found that she was hungry. She cleared her plate and had two slices of toast with butter and marmalade.

Gran said, 'A few more things about wolves, while I think of it. Don't try and stroke their heads until you've got to know them.'

'Stroke? Why would I want to stroke a wolf? Anyway, they'll be in cages, won't they?'

'Compounds. They're not shut in all the time. When we walk them—'

'You take the wolves out for a *walk*?'

'Not me personally, but the trained handlers do. The wolves go out to agricultural shows quite often in the summer. School visits are popular too.'

'Isn't that risky, taking wolves where there are small children?'

'Not at all. The wolves enjoy the attention. They're accustomed to people – the object of the exercise is to get people accustomed to them.'

'How did you get involved in all this, Gran? Are you an eco-warrior?'

'Zack's enthusiasm is infectious. He made me see wolves differently. I helped to hand rear some cubs. After you've fed a bottle of milk to a helpless handful of fur, it's difficult to think of wolves as man-eaters.'

Gran went into teacher mode and delivered a lecture that lasted through the clearing away and washing up. Anna didn't take it all in, but some of it stuck. There were two species of wolf at the sanctuary: North American and European. The North American wolves were the friendlier of the two, but weren't allowed to breed because they were too closely related. The sanctuary had inherited them from a game park in Oxfordshire that had a wolf over-population problem. The European wolves came from Romania. Zack had been told that they were used to human contact, but they turned out not to be. However, since they weren't related they'd been allowed to mate, and had produced the first cubs born in England for centuries.

There was a lot more that Anna didn't listen to, but one thing was clear: Gran didn't just know about wolves, she really cared about them; when she described the cubs, her face was soft and mumsy.

Anna couldn't figure it out.

The approach to the sanctuary was along a drive that sloped down between an avenue of oak trees. Gran parked the car on a patch of rough ground. Two other vehicles were parked there; one of them was Zack's truck.

Anna got out of the car, her heart pounding. To her

left was a hedge and beyond that a field where a mare grazed with her colt. To her right was a tall chain-link fence surrounding a grassy enclosure with a hillock at its centre. On the other side of the fence were four wolves.

Anna had thought that the wolves would be grey, but they were biscuit-coloured, brindled with black. One of the wolves lay curled up asleep on the hillock, the others were patrolling the fence, in single file.

Anna was paralysed.

'Let's meet the stars of the show,' said Gran.

The three wolves stopped pacing as Gran and Anna drew near. Their ears pricked up and their heads twitched as they sniffed the air. One wolf flattened its ears and began a peculiar, scrabbling dance.

To Anna's horror, Gran went right up to the fence and poked her fingers through the wire.

'Gran, don't!'

'It's all right, she knows me. This is Nanook. Come and say hello.'

The wolf was licking Gran's fingers and whimpering.

'Offer her the back of your hand so she can get your scent,' Gran said. 'Mind you keep your fingers closed around your thumb. If she bites, the skin on the back of your hand will be too thin for her to grip.'

Anna didn't find Gran's advice very reassuring. 'Do I have to?'

'Try it.'

Anna gingerly pushed the back of her fisted hand against the fence. Nanook dabbed her wet nose on Anna's skin and snuffled.

'Nanook is a North American wolf,' Gran explained. 'She's the pack's alpha female.'

'The what?'

'The dominant female. Only the alpha male and female breed.'

'Which is the alpha male?'

Gran pointed at the wolf on the hillock. 'Manitou. He's not as friendly as the others. They're females. The pale-faced one is Tonaq, the one with the black mask is Kannuk.'

'Weird names!'

'They're named after Native North American spirits. The European wolves have Norse gods' names.'

On one side of the fence was a long, low concrete building. At the front were doors like giant cat flaps. The doors were attached to pulleys and steel wires so that they could be raised or lowered. The back of the building was outside the fence and had a standard-sized metal door set into it. The door swung open and Zack appeared. He was wearing jeans tucked into the tops of brown army boots, and a black sweatshirt with a picture of a wolf's head printed on it.

'So there you are!' he said to Gran. 'What time d'you call this?'

'Half past eight, the same as everybody else calls it,' said Gran.

'Best part of the day's over. I've been up since five.'

'Are you boasting or complaining?'

Zack grunted. 'While you're working your fingers to the bone, washing out the den, I'm going to give your ravishing granddaughter a guided tour.' He flashed Anna a twinkly-eyed smile. 'Would you like to meet the cubs?'

'Er…' said Anna.

'This way!'

Zack led Anna past the opened door. Anna caught a smell that made her eyes water, a heady mix of ammonia and burnt bacon. She coughed and waved her hand in front of her face.

'Pungent, isn't it?' said Zack. 'Once you've smelled wolves' droppings, you never forget it.'

'I wonder why that is?'

Zack raised one eyebrow. 'You've inherited your grandmother's sarcasm, I see. Are you as stubborn as she is?'

'It all depends on who I'm with.'

'I suppose she told you about the cubs – in exhaustive detail.'

'Pretty much. She said that you'd persuaded her into helping to rear them.'

'Persuaded? We had to put up razor wire to keep her away. She did nights, giving the cubs a feed every four hours. At the end of the first week she looked like the queen of the zombies.' Zack opened a gate with a metal frame. 'Follow me inside to the next gate. Let me go into the compound first.'

'We're going *into* the compound?'

'You can't meet them if they're on the other side of the fence, can you? No need to get your undergarments in a knot, the cubs are kept separate from the adult wolves.'

When Anna passed through the second gate, her knees were trembling and breakfast had turned into a hard lump in the pit of her stomach.

A cub came lolloping towards her, looking like a

pint-sized German Shepherd. It butted its shoulder against Anna's legs, dropped to the ground, rolled over on to its back and gazed imploringly at her with its slanted amber eyes.

'You can take that as an invitation,' said Zack.

'To do what?'

'Scratch his belly.'

Anna didn't sense any hostility in the cub. She squatted on her heels and raked her fingers through the rough fur.

I'm touching a wolf, she thought. I'm actually touching a wolf.

The cub twisted its head and licked her wrist; its tongue felt warm and soapy.

The hard lump in Anna's stomach dissolved.

'What's its name?' she said.

'*His* name,' Zack corrected her. 'He's Loki. Loki was the god of mischief, so the name suits him perfectly. His sisters are Freya and Bayla. They're not as sassy as he is.'

To prove his sassiness, Loki gently closed his jaws around Anna's wrist, mock-biting, and then lunged at her face, snapping his fangs shut a few centimetres from the tip of her nose.

Anna laughed.

Thirty minutes flashed by. Anna played with the cubs and forgot that she was supposed to be afraid of wolves. She noticed how Freya and Bayla showed their subservience by lying down and letting Loki stand over them.

A lot of the play involved a bone, which Loki defended from his sisters with an alarmingly fierce growl, but he let Anna take it from him without a sound.

Zack said, 'Had enough?'

Anna hadn't had enough; she would have been happy to spend the rest of the day with the cubs.

'It's time I put Manitou in the den, so the compound can be cleaned,' said Zack.

'The alpha male?'

'My, you have been doing your homework, haven't you?'

'Doesn't he mind being shut in the den?'

'There are days when he objects, yes. Manitou can be a real handful. That's why it's my job to handle him – I can be a bit of a handful myself.'

'Is he vicious?'

'Let's say he's choosy about the company he keeps. Look.'

Zack rolled up the left sleeve of his sweatshirt. His arm was pocked with silver bite marks like lunar craters.

'He bit you?' said Anna.

'Of course he bit me, he's a bloody wolf, isn't he? I'm the one who got him used to human contact and it was a steep learning curve for us both. He's humanised, but he's not tame. None of the wolves are, and don't you ever forget it.'

'Why did you humanise him? Wouldn't he be better off living in the wild somewhere?'

'Wolves are hunted in the wild,' Zack said grimly. 'The whole point of the sanctuary is for members of the public to meet wolves and find out that they're not as dangerous as their reputation makes them out to be. That's why we do Wolf Walks and school visits. I was hoping Manitou would be the main attraction, but he's too strong and too unpredictable. He stays in the compound while the females are out walking.'

'Doesn't he get any exercise then?'

'Only on his own, and only with me,' Zack said with a note of pride in his voice.

The cubs didn't want Anna to go. They followed her to the inner gate of the compound, milling around her legs, and it took a lot of manoeuvring to slip past them.

Gran was outside the den, talking to a young man. Anna didn't pay them any attention, because Manitou had woken up and was trotting down the hillock towards the fence.

Everything else in Anna's world disappeared.

Manitou was at least a third bigger than the shewolves, with powerful muscles that worked along his back. He didn't slink but kept his head erect, ears cocked forwards.

Though Manitou was all that Anna feared in a wolf – sharp-fanged, red-tongued, hungry-eyed – she felt such a strong urge to sink her fingers into his thick coat that, without thinking, she stepped up to the fence to get closer to him.

Manitou registered her movement and came straight at her. His ears went flat and he shook his head playfully. Anna could see the cub in him and Manitou must have seen something in her, because he reared on his hind legs, hit the fence with his front paws and tried to lick her face.

Anna instinctively stepped back; Manitou whined.

'Good God alive!' muttered Zack. 'He seems to

have taken a shine to you.'

Anna felt awestruck.

Gran said, 'Anna? I'd like you to meet Pete.'

Anna turned, and her breath was taken away.

Pete was beautiful: black hair, an angular face with high cheekbones and an even tan, dark brown eyes with sweeping lashes.

'Pete is Zack's grandson,' said Gran.

'Hi,' said Anna.

Pete half-smiled and nodded, no friendliness in his eyes. There was something tense and guarded about him. Anna thought he must be shy.

'Pete gives up a lot of his time to work at the sanctuary,' said Gran. 'Zack couldn't manage without him.'

Pete shrugged the compliment off with one shoulder, and the way he did it made Anna change her mind about him – he wasn't shy, he was arrogant.

Pete said, 'Better go,' wheeled around and walked off, just like that.

How up yourself can you get? Anna thought.

Anna watched Zack put Manitou on a chain leash – or try to, anyway. Manitou literally gave Zack the run-around, circling him, standing still and then bolting away when he came near. The wolf was playing, but only just. When he curled up his top lip and snarled at Zack, he sounded as if he meant it and the snarl made the hairs on Anna's forearms prickle. She wouldn't have gone into the compound if someone offered her National Lottery roll-over money to do it.

Zack surprised Anna. She'd expected him to come out with a string of ripe swear words, but he showed incredible patience, taking care not to approach Manitou from behind, keeping the leash where the wolf could see it. Their relationship appeared to be a mixture of affection and respect.

At last, Manitou relented and let Zack slip the loop of the chain over his head. As soon as the leash was in place Manitou lunged forward, almost pulling Zack over. It was hard to decide who was in control of whom.

When Manitou was securely denned, Pete entered the compound and helped Zack to put away the she wolves. They went without fuss. Nanook was the last to go, and when Pete put her on the leash she yapped excitedly and nuzzled his palm.

Anna gave Gran a hand cleaning the compound – not the world's most appealing or pleasant-smelling job, but she couldn't stand around watching Gran do it on her own. After they left the compound, Zack turned a crank handle that operated the doors. Manitou was first out. He bounded over to Anna and pressed his flank against the fence, growling softly – a strikingly gentle sound for such a big animal.

'He likes you,' said Gran.

'Oh, sure he does!' said Anna.

But as the morning went on, Anna began to think that Gran might be right. Whenever she passed the compound, Manitou kept pace with her, as if he were stalking her. It was creepy.

And Manitou wasn't the only one interested in Anna. While she was working with Gran, cleaning the European wolves' compound, Anna caught Pete gazing at her from the far side of the sanctuary. He turned away before their eyes met, and Anna thought that he was blushing, but couldn't be sure. Not that it mattered; whatever Pete's problem was, she didn't want any.

Gran finished at one o'clock. As Anna was getting into

the car, she saw Manitou sitting close to the fence, staring at her. He threw back his head and let out a howl.

'What's wrong with him, Gran?' said Anna.

'You are,' Gran said. 'He howls when the females go off without him. I think he's in love.'

Anna shivered with revulsion, but at the same time felt a thrill of pride. The combination made her curious.

7

After lunch, back at Gran's, Anna decided to read up on wolves. Gran had a folder of pamphlets and information sheets that the sanctuary issued to its members, and Anna worked her way through it while Gran carried on with the cat portrait.

The contents of the folder were an eye-opener; Anna discovered that most of what she'd believed about wolves was nowhere near the truth. Wolves didn't howl at the full moon – nobody was exactly sure why they howled, the best guess being that it was a way of claiming territory and finding a mate. Big packs were rare, wolves usually hunted in family groups of five or six. They weren't a threat to farmers: surveys done in the USA revealed that less than one per cent of livestock losses were down to wolves.

But the biggest surprise was that wolves were no danger to humans. There were no records of wolves attacking people in the States, and the rare European attacks had been carried out by wolves with rabies. The Big Bad Wolf turned out to be intelligent, timid and nothing like as great a threat to humans as humans were to him. All over the world wolves were snared, shot and poisoned because of a deep-rooted fear that had no basis in reality. People killed wolves as though they had a natural right; they didn't understand anything about the animals they were destroying.

The most shocking thing Anna found in the pamphlets was a photograph. Two men stood in front of a wooden cabin in a snowy landscape. The men were bearded, wore old-fashioned clothes and carried rifles. They looked pleased with themselves. Behind them, a long line of dead wolves were hanging from the eaves of the cabin; more wolves lay in piles on the veranda.

Twelve hours previously, the photograph would have meant nothing to Anna; now it appalled her. If Manitou had been alive then, he might have ended up dangling on a rope from the roof of the cabin. Anna was outraged: she feared Manitou, but he didn't deserve to die because of it; the fear was *her* problem.

All fired-up, Anna marched into the conservatory and said, 'I want to get involved.'

Gran didn't stop painting. 'With what?' she said.

'The sanctuary. How do I join?'

'The annual membership fee is twenty-five pounds.'

'I'm not talking about money, I want to *do* something.'

Gran pushed her reading glasses on to her forehead and smiled knowingly, like she was one step ahead. 'Your sudden conversion wouldn't have anything to do with Pete, would it?'

'Pete?'

'He's an attractive lad.'

Anna was irritated – what did Pete have to do with anything?

'Yeah,' she said, 'but he's also a jerk.'

'Not when you get to know him.'

'I can't spare the time – too many interesting things to do.'

'If you say so. I'm sure Zack could find something for you. He's always complaining about being short-handed. I warn you, the work won't be glamorous.'

'I don't care.'

'Zack's a demanding taskmaster.'

'I can handle Zack.'

Gran laughed. 'Don't you believe it! Zack's bite is worse than his bark, especially where females are concerned.'

'Alpha male, huh?'

'Reactionary old sexist, more like. Still, if you're serious, give him a call. His number's on the Rolodex next to the phone. Look under H for Hebron.'

The phone rang for ages before someone picked it up.

'Hello?'

Anna frowned; it wasn't Zack.

'Hello,' she said. 'Could I speak to Mr Hebron, please?'

'He's not available. Can I take a message?'

Anna placed the voice. 'Is that Pete?'

'Yeah.'

'This is Anna. We met this morning, remember?'

'Yeah.'

'I'd like to volunteer to work at the sanctuary.'

'Doing what?'

'Whatever. I don't mind.'

'When are you available?'

'Tomorrow?'

'Be here by eight thirty.'

Pete hung up.

Anna looked at the purring receiver and said, 'Thanks, it was nice talking to you too.'

Anna told Gran what Pete had said, and Gran promptly turned into the Organiser from Hell. 'I'll drop you off. I have to go to the gallery tomorrow to discuss my exhibition. I won't be able to pick you up until four.'

'OK.'

'You can borrow my spare dungarees. Take a pair of gardening gloves, in case.'

'Yes, Gran.'

'You'll have to wear your hair up. Did you bring any hair ties with you?'

'Yes, Gran.'

'Oh, packed lunch! I've got cheese, but you'd better get another sliced loaf out of the freezer.'

'Yes, Gran.'

'Remember, no perfume.'

'No, Gran.'

'Your shampoo is rather heavily scented, I noticed. There's a bottle of neutral shampoo in the bathroom. Be sure to wash your hair with that.'

'I will, Gran.'

'Now what else, I wonder?'

'Clean underwear, hankie, wash behind my ears?'

Gran blinked coldly. 'It always pays to be well prepared, Anna. You never know what may happen.'

'If you don't know what's going to happen, how can you prepare for it?'

'Assume the worst – then you can only be pleasantly surprised.'

Anna thought about it; it seemed reasonable.

Before she went to sleep, Anna flicked through Gran's copy of *The Complete Wolf*. The text was dry and technical, with plenty of statistical tables that were strictly for anoraks, but the photographs and diagrams were impressive, and the section on mating was hardcore wolf porn.

When her eyelids started to droop, Anna turned off the bedside lamp, settled down on her left side, then sat up with a start.

She'd gone the whole day without thinking about

Matt; she'd been so fazed by the sanctuary that he'd entirely slipped her mind. Did that mean she was being disloyal?

Blushing with guilt, Anna switched on the light, grabbed her notebook and a pen and wrote.

Today was weird. I met the wolves – well a wolf actually. There were other wolves around but he was the important one. His name's Manitou. I wish you could have been there, Matt. It was frightening and exciting and…I don't know how to explain it. Manitou is dangerous but beautiful – like the danger is part of the beauty.

I used to think Alsatians were like wolves, but they're not. Wolves have a completely different personality. I don't want to be frightened of them any more. Fear is what makes people kill wolves, and I'm not a wolf killer.

Manitou has a thing for me – he wants to be near me all the time. Gran reckons it's love. I don't know, I guess wolf love is pretty violent.

I can hear you saying, 'Here she goes again – another cause, like saving the environment!' It's the same thing, I suppose. Wolves have a job to do in the wild, and if we exterminate them the whole system will be thrown off balance, and the planet will suffer.

I shouldn't be writing this now. It's late, I'm tired and I'm not making a lot of sense, am I?

But I have to overcome the thing inside that makes me afraid of wolves. If I can do that, I can do anything.

8

Gran kept it up right to the last minute. She parked the car at the kerb, rummaged in her handbag, took out a piece of paper and thrust it at Anna.

'What's this?' Anna asked.

'My mobile phone number – in case of emergencies.'

'Gra-an!'

'I'm responsible for you, Anna. I'll feel easier if I know that you can contact me.'

'I'm going to be OK.'

'So am I, as long as I know you've got those numbers. I'm a neurotic old fusspot – indulge me!'

Anna gave in, pocketed the piece of paper, gave Gran a kiss on the cheek and got out of the car.

It was the first time that Anna had been on her own

since the train journey. She'd been crumpled then, now she felt as though she were regaining her shape. She walked down the lane, through the splashes of sunlight that shone between the branches of the oak trees.

Manitou was waiting in the same place, in the same pose as when she'd last seen him. He greeted her by leaping up on the fence and yapping; the top of her head was level with his throat. Anna stepped back; her insides felt as though they'd twisted into knots.

'He's trying to dominate you,' said a voice.

It was Zack; Anna hadn't heard him come up behind her.

'He wants you to react like a she wolf,' said Zack. 'You're supposed to lie down and fawn over him.'

'He's out of luck. I don't do fawning.'

'Ah, so you're a feminist?'

'No, but I live in the twenty-first century, so I don't buy into the dominant male thing.'

'You think that women should wear the trousers?'

'I think people should wear what they like.'

Zack gazed affectionately at Manitou. 'Wolves take a more instinctive approach to life. The alpha male is boss and the alpha female's function is to bear and nurture the next generation. It's a simple but effective strategy. Humans could learn a lot from it. Humans waste a lot of time denying things that ought to come naturally.'

Anna suspected that Zack was trying to wind her up, and decided not to let him.

'What d'you want me to do?' she said.

Zack strode away from the compound; Anna fell into step beside him.

'It's a busy day for us tomorrow,' Zack said. 'We're taking Nanook, Tonaq and Kannuk for a walk with two dozen members who've taken out subscriptions to the sanctuary. They'll come back here for a look around, and we give them the hard sell – posters, cuddly toys, that sort of thing. A vanload of merchandising arrived yesterday afternoon and it needs sorting out.'

'But I thought—'

'What?'

'That I'd be doing something to help the wolves.'

'You *are* helping them. Every penny we make from sales goes towards the upkeep of this place. Conserving wolves is an expensive business.'

Zack and Anna walked up a tarmac driveway to a

big wooden hut. Past the hut was a neatly-mowed lawn and a two-storey house with a pantiled roof. Pete was outside the hut, stripping a protective polythene sheet from a stack of cardboard boxes.

'Pete will show you the ropes,' said Zack. 'I've got calls to make. A film company wants to hire a wolf for an advertisement.'

'What are they advertising?'

'Soap.'

'What have wolves got to do with soap?'

Zack turned the palms of his hands up to the sky. 'Who knows? They promised not to show the wolf in a negative way and offered a fat fee, so I didn't like to ask.' He left Anna with Pete and walked towards the house.

Pete acted like Anna wasn't there. He didn't say hello and kept his back to her as he folded the polythene.

Anna waited until her impatience got the better of her. 'I could help you with that,' she said.

'I can manage,' Pete said.

'Then tell me what needs doing. Believe it or not, watching you wrestle with a sheet of plastic isn't all that interesting.'

Pete gave Anna a sharp look over his shoulder. He stepped into the hut and came out with a clipboard that had a biro attached to it with string. 'Here's the inventory. Check the items in the cardboard boxes and tick them off. If anything's missing, tell me or Zack.'

'Is that all?'

'No. Unpack the boxes and put the stuff on the shelves in the hut. It's mostly T-shirts and sweatshirts. Arrange them according to size. The shelves are already labelled, so you shouldn't have any problem. Think you can hack it?'

'Yes.'

'I'll be around the compound somewhere if you need me.'

Don't hold your breath! Anna thought.

It was a shame that Pete was so condescending; it cancelled out his good looks.

Anna opened boxes, ticked the inventory and loaded shelves. The shirts had pictures of wolves on them, and phrases like *Spirits of the Forest* and *The Call of the Wild*. They came in Small, Medium, Large and Extra Large.

The interior of the hut was dank and cobwebby. The metal shelves were fixed with screws and wing nuts. Whoever had written the labels had terrible handwriting, but once Anna managed to decipher the scrawl, her task was straightforward – if boring. She guessed that she'd be seeing wolf T-shirts in her dreams.

The last box she opened was marked Mouse Mats. Anna thought it must be a mistake, then saw that the mats were printed with a photograph of Manitou – a close-up of his head, jaws open, tongue lolling.

Pete came up the drive, with his hands deep in his pockets and his shoulders slumped. Whatever he had on his mind gave him a vulnerable look, and Anna realised that he wasn't as old as she'd thought – seventeen, eighteen, maybe.

'Finished?' Pete said.

'Almost. I just have to count these and put them away. How much d'you charge for them?'

'Five fifty.'

Anna reached into her pocket for her purse. 'Do I pay you or Zack?'

'Take one if you want one. You've earned it.'

'I'd rather pay.'

Anna handed Pete the money.

'Any glitches?' Pete said.

'Nope.'

'I'll do the rest. You can take a lunch break.'

'After I've dealt with this lot.'

'Suit yourself.'

Pete made to go.

Anna said, 'Mind telling me something, Pete?'

'What?'

'Is it me in particular you don't like, or is it girls in general?'

Pete frowned. 'What makes you ask that?'

'Your attitude. Don't you think it would make life more pleasant if we were polite to each other?'

Pete wriggled his shoulders. 'I'm sorry if you think I've been rude. I didn't mean to be. It's just…I prefer working on my own, you know?'

Pete was lying, Anna could tell. There was something he wanted to protect, a place he wouldn't let anyone else into. For some reason he changed his mind about going, and hung around while Anna counted the mouse mats. When she went to shelve them, he followed her into the hut and gave her efforts a once-over.

'Good job,' he said.

'Thanks.'

'How are you fixed for tomorrow?'

'Tomorrow?'

'It's members' day. We have two stalls, one for merchandising, one for refreshments. I'm in charge of them both. It gets pretty hectic running between the two. I could use some help.'

'Don't tell me, let me guess,' said Anna. 'I'm a girl, so you want me to make the tea and coffee. Am I right?'

She was right, but Pete wasn't going to let on. 'Sell merchandise if you'd rather. I'd just appreciate a hand, that's all. You don't have to if you don't want to.'

'I'll be here. I don't mind doing the refreshments. I was just being awkward.'

'Why?'

'Because the best way to get along with you and Zack is to be a stroppy cow, isn't it?'

Pete smiled a real smile. It made Anna think that if she hadn't already met him, if he were a stranger she'd seen at a party or in a club, she would have looped the loop to get a smile like that from him.

Anna ate her cheese sandwiches at the compound, watching Manitou watching her. His eyes followed her every movement, as though he was as curious about her as she was about him. Sharing his company was oddly relaxing, and when she'd finished eating, Anna risked going close to the fence.

Manitou jumped up again, but Anna held her fist to the wire, at waist height.

'You're going to have to come down to my level, big boy,' she said.

Manitou dropped on all fours, flattened his ears, gave Anna's knuckles a fleeting lick and then backed away, growling.

'Tough guy, huh?' Anna said. 'You want to get to know me, but you hate letting it show.'

She wondered if it was a wolf thing or a male thing.

Gran was on time. Zack just happened to appear at the same moment as Gran, and walked over to the car with Anna. Gran rolled down her window and Zack leaned against the sill.

'Can you spare Anna tomorrow, Joanna?' he said. 'She's offered to be tea lady.'

'You mean working one day with you wasn't enough? She must have a masochistic streak.'

'Please, Gran,' said Anna, 'I promised.'

'If it's all right with you, it's all right with me. What time do you want her, Zack?'

'About two. Don't bother to come and pick her up, Pete or I will give her a lift back.' Zack straightened up and rested his hands on his hips. 'When are you going to ask me around to cook you a decent meal again, woman? You're nothing but a bag of bones.'

'I'll take a rain check,' said Gran. 'Perhaps after Anna's holiday is over.'

'You'll starve before then. Besides, Anna's longing to sample my cooking, aren't you, Anna?'

'Er…'

'That's settled then. Tomorrow evening.' Zack turned to Gran. 'Have you got any prawns?'

'Yes.'

'I'll do you a prawn curry.'

Gran moaned in delight. 'You know I can't resist your prawn curries.'

'Stop pretending, woman!' Zack said with a chuckle. 'It's me you can't resist.'

Gran said casually, 'Why don't you bring Pete along, if he's at a loose end? He'll be company for Anna.'

'I'll ask him,' said Zack, equally casually.

It had *set-up* written all over it. Anna was about to object, but Manitou interrupted her by howling.

'I'd better go and pay him some attention,' said

Zack. 'See you tomorrow, Anna. Thanks for your help today.'

'You're welcome.'

Anna was seething. She got into the car and said, 'What's going on, Gran?'

'Nothing.'

'What's with inviting Pete over for dinner?'

Gran sniffed. 'You seem to forget that it's my house, Anna. I'll invite whom I like to it, if it's all the same to you.'

And that was that – subject closed.

9

Anna hadn't been shopping since the day she arrived at Gran's. On a normal Saturday she'd spend an hour or so hanging out at the mall with Maggie, but this Saturday, shopping with Gran in a hypermarket on the outskirts of town, came as a shock to the system. The car park was vast and smelled of exhaust fumes; the hypermarket looked like a church; the aisles were crowded with blank-eyed people; the air was bland with muzak. The bright packaging dazzled Anna's eyes and the range of products on offer made her giddy. She was hemmed in, inhaling recycled breath, seeing in artificial light; her body space was constantly invaded by people leaning over her to grab what they wanted from the shelves.

It was a relief to escape and get back to Gran's.

Gran wouldn't let Anna put anything away. 'I know just where everything goes,' she said. 'Telling you where to put things would take longer than doing it myself.'

So Anna stood and watched as Gran restocked the cupboards.

'Who was your first love, Gran?'

Gran narrowed her eyes suspiciously. 'Why do you want to know – are you doing a project on ancient history?'

'No, personal research.'

'I can't honestly remember. I went to a convent school, so contact with males was rather limited. Boys were a mystery, a bit intimidating. As for sex, it wasn't mentioned much in the Fifties. It was something that rabbits did in Biology textbooks.'

'When did you first—I mean, who did you—'

'The first person I had sex with was Gordon Martin. I met him at university when I was nineteen.'

'What was he like?'

'At the time, or looking back?'

'There's a difference?'

'A great deal of difference. At the time, I thought he was a rebel because he dressed in black, wore a beret, listened to modern jazz and wrote poetry. Looking back, he was a pretentious poser and his poetry stank. God knows what I ever saw in him.'

'Were you in love?'

'I fooled myself into thinking that I was, but it wasn't love. To tell you the truth, I went to bed with him because I was curious – and scared that if I didn't, I'd end up a spinster.'

'At nineteen?'

Gran laughed. 'Like most teenagers, I was in a rush to grow up. In my day that meant getting married and having children, so I did, but it didn't make me feel any more grown-up than I felt when I was nineteen.'

'What happened to Gordon?'

'He passed on to the next girl who was eager to lose her virginity. The last I heard of him, he was an editor at the BBC.'

Anna frowned. 'I could never talk to Mum and Dad about stuff like this, it would be too embarrassing. Why isn't it embarrassing to talk to you?'

'Because I'm too old to have any shame.'

Anna startled herself by saying, 'Gran, d'you think that what Matt and I did was wrong?'

'I think that before you commit yourself to

anything, you should be fully aware of what the consequences might be.'

'Is that a yes or a no?'

'Both.'

Anna thought, Consequences? How can love have consequences? It's…it's…

But without Matt there in front of her, it was difficult for Anna to define what love was.

Gran drove Anna to the sanctuary at two o'clock. Volunteers that Anna hadn't seen before were bustling about with brooms and pails. Pete was interacting with Manitou. Manitou was pacing nervously, stopping to lick Pete's hand through the fence, then darting away, playing hard to get.

'What's with him?' said Anna.

'He's stressed because the she wolves aren't here. They're out on the walk.'

'Doesn't he ever go with them?'

Pete shook his head. 'Zack says Manitou is too boisterous. When Zack takes him for a walk, he won't even let me go along.'

'You live with Zack?'

'At the moment. Dad's on a five-year contract in

Saudi Arabia. It was either move in with Zack, or boarding school.'

'What about your mum?'

'She's dead.'

'Oh, I'm sorry.'

'It's OK, it wasn't your fault. So it's just me, Zack and the wolves, which suits me fine.'

'No mates?'

'A couple.'

'Girlfriend?'

Pete switched off. 'Let's get going,' he said. 'The visitors will be here in half an hour.'

Anna and Pete erected trestle tables, a large one for the merchandise and a smaller one for refreshments. They hung samples of the T-shirts and sweatshirts on a portable clothes rack, brought out a display of photographs of wolves and some iffy posters of paintings that made wolves look twee and safe; then fridge magnets, key rings, pencils, erasers, hologram stickers.

'People *buy* this tack?' said Anna.

'You bought a mouse mat, didn't you?'

'That's different. I wanted a picture of Manitou.'

Pete did a wickedly accurate imitation of Zack. 'I see you go for the macho type.'

'I don't have a type,' Anna said coldly. 'I take people as they are and one at a time.'

'It was a joke!' said Pete. 'I didn't mean—'

He didn't get the chance to finish what he was saying, because the first wave of visitors arrived.

They were all ages, shapes and sizes, and all slightly delirious, like they'd been through an experience that they weren't quite over. It put them in the mood for shopping.

Anna had just about regained her breath when the second wave descended: more teas and coffees; so many ten-pound notes that she was forced to borrow change from Pete. When they'd bought everything they wanted, the visitors hung around, reluctant to leave. Eventually Zack rounded them up and herded them off. He bagged the takings while Pete and Anna put the stock and the tables away.

Pete padlocked the door of the hut, leaned his back against it and let out a long sigh. 'Congratulations, Anna – we survived!'

'Only just. Are the visitors always so blissed out?'

'Pretty much. You get the occasional one who freaks because their wolf phobia is stronger than they thought, but most people come back from the Wolf

Walk in a trance.' Pete looked at his watch. 'Oops! I'd better drive you home.'

'Can I check on Manitou before we go?'

'Sure.'

Manitou was busy asserting himself after his reunion with the she wolves. He went from one to the other and stood over them, lowering his muzzle so that they could lick it.'

'Look at him!' said Anna. 'He's in Wolf Heaven, surrounded by adoring females.'

'But he can't mate with them because they're his sisters. We have to put him in a separate compound during the mating season.'

'When's that?'

'February and March. Manitou doesn't like being on his own. He howls a lot.'

'Couldn't you bring another she wolf in for him to breed with? I'd love to see his pups.'

'We've got enough wolves as it is,' Pete said. 'We can't afford to keep any more. Manitou will have to put up with being celibate for the time being.'

Anna thought: Love, but no sex. She said, 'I know how he feels.'

'Me too.'

Anna wanted to ask Pete what he meant, but left it. Working together had made a kind of bond between them, but it was too fragile to take any strain. Though Pete wasn't a stranger any more, Anna still didn't know him.

Zack and Pete turned up at seven fifteen. Zack was wearing a safari suit. Pete had on a grey roll-neck sweater, black jeans and white trainers; his newly-washed hair was soft and shiny.

Gran had changed into black ski-pants and a white blouse with the collar turned up. Her gold leather belt should have looked naff, but Gran managed to get away with it.

Zack gave Gran a bottle of wine and a peck on the cheek. 'You're looking particularly splendid tonight, Joanna – not a day over sixty,' he said. 'What say we ditch the youngsters, get drunk and let nature take its course?'

'If we do, you'll fall asleep on the sofa and I'll fall asleep in an armchair, until your snoring wakes me up.'

Zack made a face. 'Where's your sense of romance, woman?'

'Safely locked away, where it belongs.'

'We'll see about that! The night is young and I'm an expert lock-picker.'

The banter continued into the kitchen. Zack and Gran did a comedy routine where he was the temperamental chef and she was the clumsy assistant. They traded insults, as usual, but it suddenly struck Anna that their insults were a way of flirting with each other. She felt as though she were eavesdropping, and tried to start a conversation with Pete to distract herself.

They talked about school and didn't get very far: Pete was in the Sixth Form, studying sciences; he wanted to be a vet. Anna wasn't interested in science and didn't know what career she wanted.

After school fizzled out, they switched to music. Another brick wall: Anna liked techno, Pete was into country and western.

'Songs about orphans and dogs?' said Anna.

'At least the songs are about something. Techno sounds like robots breaking wind in the bath.'

'It's brilliant to dance to.'

'I'll take your word for it. I don't go dancing any more.'

'But you used to?'

'I wasn't any good at it. Susie said—' Pete flinched.

'Susie?'

'This girl I used to know.'

'What did she say?'

'Forget it. It doesn't matter.'

But it obviously did matter.

Just as things were about to get awkward, Zack came to the rescue by announcing that dinner was ready.

The food was delicious. Zack kept up a stream of stories about visitors to the sanctuary, that made everybody laugh; Gran countered with anecdotes about teaching; Pete and Anna hardly said a word.

Anna passed on dessert. 'I'm stuffed,' she said. 'I'm going to stroll round the garden to walk it off. Won't be long.'

She went out through the conservatory, on to the patio. The garden was black and silver in the moonlight. Anna slipped off her sandals and walked on to the lawn, kneading the grass with her toes. She was real again; she'd lost herself for a while in all the hassle over Matt, played the part of a tragic heroine in a doomed love affair so well that she'd begun to forget who she was; now she was back. Being away from

Matt, her friends and parents, and the routine of living at home had given her a new take on herself. Meeting the wolves had shown her that there was more to life than boyfriends, shopping and gossip.

Anna turned in the direction of the sanctuary and tried to reach out through the dark to Manitou. Maybe he was asleep in his den, brush curled round his nose, dreaming whatever it was that wolves dreamed of. She envied him – he didn't have to worry about right and wrong, or make plans for the future.

Anna howled softly.

Pete stepped out on to the patio.

Anna hoped that he hadn't heard the howl. 'Did Gran and Zack drive you away?' she asked.

'They're into teaching reminiscences,' said Pete. 'I felt surplus to requirements.'

He joined Anna on the lawn.

Anna held her arms out, hugging the night. 'I love it here. I didn't want to come and stay with Gran, but I'm glad that I did.'

'If you didn't want to stay with Jo, what are you doing here?'

'My parents made me.'

'Why?'

'Family problems.'

Pete nodded, but didn't pry. 'Zack was impressed with the work you put in today,' he said. 'He wants you to go on the Wolf Walk tomorrow morning, as a reward.'

'I'd love to!'

'Pick you up about ten o'clock?'

'Great! Thanks, Pete.'

'Don't thank me,' said Pete. 'It was Zack's idea.'

It was gone eleven by the time Zack and Pete left. Gran poured herself the last dribble of wine, reclined on the sofa and said, 'That went off rather well.'

'Yes,' said Anna. 'Zack's good company, isn't he?'

'When he wants to be. What did you and Pete get up to in the garden?'

'Nothing. He's taking me on a Wolf Walk tomorrow morning.'

'You still think he's a jerk?'

'Yes, but not as big a jerk as I first thought.'

Gran drank her wine. 'You and Pete have got a lot in common.'

'We've got nothing in common! The guy listens to country and western music!'

'You've both been hurt.'

'Who hasn't?'

'Who indeed?'

Anna waited for Gran to go on; when Gran didn't, Anna gave her a prod. 'What hurt?'

'Pardon?'

'You told me Pete had been hurt – how?'

'That's not for me to say.'

'Then why mention it?'

Gran yawned. 'I shouldn't drink wine, it makes me run off at the mouth. Don't pay any attention to what I say when I'm squiffy.'

Anna frowned – she had the strangest feeling that Gran was nowhere near as squiffy as she was making out.

10

Anna's alarm clock woke her at eight. She turned on her side and looked at the photo of her and Matt, like she did every morning. This time something was different about it. Anna picked up the photograph and inspected it closely.

She was the same – snuggling into Matt's chest, big grin like the cat that had got the cream, eyes that said, 'He's mine – keep off!' Matt was grinning too, but now Anna noticed how stiff the grin was. Matt's eyes had an uncertain expression in them, as if he'd got himself into a situation that he didn't know how to deal with.

Anna remembered the day the photograph was taken. She and Matt were waiting for a train, she spotted the photo booth and hauled Matt over to it.

Matt kept saying no, his hair wasn't right, he had a zit coming on his cheek – Anna wouldn't listen. She steamrollered him. She wanted evidence that they were a couple, something she could show her mates to make them jealous.

Listening to Gran analyse her relationship with Grandad had rubbed off on Anna, and she indulged in a little analysis of her own. Love was supposed to be about sharing and consideration, but Anna had only considered herself. She'd pestered Matt into saying he loved her, because she wanted to know what it felt like to hear it.

It had been more like manipulation than love.

Gran was in the conservatory, concentrating on the cat painting, giving off strong Do Not Disturb vibes. Anna brewed a pot of tea in the kitchen and ate a bowl of cereal with yoghurt and a sliced apple.

Gran called out, 'I've finished! Come and tell me what you think.'

Anna leaned on the frame of the conservatory door and stared at the painting: a black and white long-haired cat with a red bow tie around its neck, crouched on a blue satin cushion. It was copied from a photograph that the cat's owner had taken as a joke, but there was nothing joky about Gran's painting; the cat looked serene and dignified.

'Well?' said Gran.

'It's good.'

'Good?'

'It's a really catty-looking cat.'

'That was the intention.'

Gran wanted reassurance; Anna thought harder and said, 'I don't know anything about art, but if I'd paid you for that painting, I'd be pleased with it.'

Gran seemed satisfied; she dipped a rag in white spirit and scrubbed at the splashes of paint on her hands.

'You ought to paint the wolves, Gran,' said Anna. 'You could do better than those posters they sell at the sanctuary.'

'I should hope I could! Actually, I did do some sketches at one point. I intended to have them printed up as cards, but I never got round to it.'

'Can I see them?'

'Certainly.'

Gran rummaged behind a filing cabinet and pulled out a sketchbook. 'There you are.'

The first drawings were clumsy, too many lines and

too much heavy shading; Gran hadn't got the wolves' proportions right, their legs were too long on one page, too short on the next. The margins were filled with studies of wolves' heads, scribbled through. The later sketches were better: Anna recognised Nanook and Tonaq; Gran had managed to capture their personalities as well as their shapes.

The final drawing grabbed Anna and wouldn't let go – Manitou standing on the hillock, front legs slightly splayed, one flowing line stretching from the tip of his nose to the tip of his brush, ears pricked, mouth closed. All of Manitou was in it: pride, aloofness, loneliness; essence of wolf.

'It's him, Gran!' Anna gasped.

'You like it?'

'More than like! Is it for sale?'

'No, but you can have it as a gift.'

Anna gave Gran a hug. 'Thanks, Gran. You're the best.'

'Nice to know that someone thinks so.'

It didn't sound like an offhand remark.

'You OK, Gran?'

'Perfectly. The portrait is finished, you're impressed with my drawing – what else could an old woman want?'

'You're not old.'

'Yes I am.'

'Not inside you're not.'

Gran smiled ruefully. 'I don't suppose anybody is, inside. That's the trouble, our bodies age faster than the rest of us.'

'Meaning?'

'Meaning that I've got a mild hangover and I should take some aspirin.'

But it was more than a hangover that Gran had and it was nothing that aspirin could cure.

Pete arrived in a yellow and red 2CV, with its canvas hood rolled back. It looked like a big toy.

'What's that?' said Anna, closing the front door behind her.

Pete rubbed his nose. 'Um, my car? Zack bought it for me after I passed my test. Manky, isn't it?'

'I think it's cute.'

Pete shrugged. 'It goes.'

'Then let's go somewhere in it.'

Pete drove towards the sanctuary, then turned off on to a side road.

'Where are we going?' Anna asked.

'Hencham Wood. It's a Forestry Commission place.'

'How many visitors are you expecting?'

'Twenty or so.'

Pete's voice was clipped and reserved. He was blowing cool again, like he wasn't comfortable with Anna's being there.

'What side of the bed did you get out on this morning?' Anna said.

'Huh?'

'You're a bit distant.'

'I'm nervous about the walk,' said Pete. 'It's always dodgy when the wolves meet the public. People go over the top and act like the wolves are tame. Sometimes they get nipped and kick up a fuss. One guy said he was going to sue the sanctuary, but Zack talked him down.'

'Has anyone been bitten?'

'Not yet, but when you put wolves and people together, you never can tell.'

Anna wasn't convinced by Pete's explanation of his frostiness, but gave him the benefit of the doubt. She thought that they'd begun to relax with each other, now they seemed to be back to square one. Anna filed her doubts away for future reference; she was too excited about the walk to pay much attention to anything else.

Pete pulled in at a section of road where other vehicles were parked. People dressed in outdoor gear – waterproof jackets and walking boots – were standing around chatting. Their ages ran from ten to seventy. Some were laughing too loudly, like they were nervous; others were silent, speaking only when spoken to. Anna guessed that they were as apprehensive about meeting the wolves as she'd been the first time.

Pete called the group together, led them to a path lined with fir trees and went through all the rules that Gran had drilled into Anna. Anna grasped the reasoning behind some of them: like not squatting down to greet the wolves, because they'd take it as an invitation to dominate.

Zack's truck cruised past the end of the lane, with a trailer fixed to the back.

Pete said, 'Please wait here until the wolves are unloaded. When the handlers bring them here, stand still and don't approach the wolves. Let them come to you.'

For the next two minutes, the atmosphere in the

lane changed from anticipation to something like dread.

Then the wolves appeared among the fir trees, sunlight and shadow dappling their coats, panting hoarsely as they strained against the chain leashes. Pete had Nanook, Zack had Tonaq; Kannuk's handler was George, one of the volunteer workers Anna had seen around the sanctuary.

The wolves lunged around the group, licking and sniffing, tails thrashing excitedly. People cooed in delight, surprised by the wolves' gentleness. Cameras clicked and whirred.

After a short while Nanook got bored and lurched off down the path, towing Pete behind her; the other she wolves followed her; the visitors drew out into a straggling line.

Anna walked beside Zack, taking in details. Tonaq sniffed at everything, lost in the flood of information coming in through her senses.

Every once in a while Nanook would assert herself over her sisters, lifting her tail and growling at them until they laid back their ears and lowered their heads.

'Makes a change from clearing out the compound, eh?' Zack said.

'It's a shame you have to keep them on leashes,' said Anna.

'If we didn't, they'd be off like a shot and we'd have a hell of a job getting them back!' Zack lowered his voice. 'To be honest with you, I don't much relish this part – parading the wolves like circus animals – but it alters people's minds and generates most of our cash. Taking Manitou out is more like it. I can see how he relates to his environment.'

'I wish I could go with you,' Anna said enviously.

'Get away with you!' Zack snorted. 'You don't want to be around old duffers like Manitou and me.'

Walking with the wolves was special in a way that Anna hadn't been expecting; she felt relaxed, almost tranquil. It wasn't because of anything the wolves did – they weren't cute, they didn't perform tricks – it was the feeling of being with animals that belonged in the world around them. The wolves blended with the environment in a way that human beings had forgotten. The visitors seemed to sense and respect this; they talked to one another in hushed voices, as though they were in church.

They halted for a photo call at the side of a small lake. The wolves went straight into the water.

The visitors pestered Zack with questions, which left Anna feeling out of it, so she went over to talk to Pete.

'No problems so far,' she said.

'Everybody's behaving themselves,' said Pete. 'No idiots, thank goodness.'

Hooves thudded nearby. The wolves instantly tensed, turning their heads and slanting their ears. A rider came out of the trees at the far side of the lake; the wolves watched intently until the horse went out of sight. It only took a few seconds, but it made Anna realise that, no matter how well-behaved the wolves were, just under the surface they were still wild animals with a strong instinct to hunt.

There were more photo calls along the way. Pete gradually defrosted and became more chatty.

'This is strange,' he said. 'I had myself pegged as a city boy – strictly concrete and neon, you know? Living with Zack changed all that.'

'I know what you mean,' said Anna. 'I went shopping with Gran yesterday morning, and it was a nightmare. When I first got here, I couldn't wait to go home. Now I'm not sure that I'll want to leave.'

'You'll be glad to see your friends again. Give it a

couple of days and you'll forget about this place.'

'I don't think so. Meeting the wolves has been good for me. When I think of all the dangers they have to face from humans, they make my problems look kind of trivial.'

'Boyfriend problems?' said Pete.

Anna was taken aback. 'Who's been talking about me?' she demanded.

'No one. I recognised the signs. I've been there.'

'Susie?'

Pete hesitated for a moment, then said, 'She was really something else – loud, off-the-wall sense of humour. I couldn't figure why she bothered with me, we were so different. It was that opposites attract thing.'

'What went wrong?'

Pete grimaced. 'You don't want to hear about it, and I don't want to talk about it here,' he said, jerking his head in the direction of the visitors.

Anna thought Pete was telling her to mind her own business. 'No need to get shirty, I was only making conversation.'

Pete grunted. 'Sorry,' he said. 'I'm not much use when it comes to small talk.'

'Tell me about it!' Anna muttered under her breath.

*

The end of the walk came too quickly for the visitors and the wolves. Tonaq threw a paddy: as soon as she caught sight of the trailer, she lay down on the ground and refused to budge. Zack and George had to pick her up and carry her.

When the wolves had been secured in the trailer, Zack turned to Anna and said, 'We're going back to the sanctuary. Pete will drive you back to Joanna's.'

'I'll come with you,' said Anna. 'I could help with the refreshments.'

'That's taken care of. Wait by Pete's car, will you? I want to have a quick word with him.'

As it turned out, Zack had several quick words with Pete. Pete listened with his head lowered. Zack seemed to be encouraging him to do something, and Anna wondered what it was.

On the drive back to Gran's, Pete was edgy and didn't say much. Anna thought he was in a mood and left him alone, but he suddenly surprised her by saying, 'I thought I might go see a movie tonight.'

'What's on?'

'That American high-school comedy that's getting all the hype.'

'The gross one? A whole bunch of us were going to see it, but I wound up at Gran's instead.'

'I'll take you, if you still want to go,' Pete said gruffly.

Anna didn't think she'd heard right. 'Sorry?'

'I'll take you to the movie.'

'You're asking me out on a *date*?'

Pete flinched. 'Definitely not! It's just, I'm on my own, you're on your own, and it's more fun watching movies with someone.'

Anna lightened up. Pete wasn't coming on to her – in fact, as far as she could tell, he didn't like her that much – and the alternative was Sunday night TV with Gran.

'Yeah, why not? What time?'

'Seven o'clock.'

Pete sounded as though he were booking a dental appointment.

'Thanks for asking me. I could do with a laugh,' Anna said, though she wasn't entirely certain that Pete was the kind of person she could have a laugh with. He was a tough guy to figure, friendly one minute, surly and moody the next. If Anna hadn't found Pete so irritating, she would have been intrigued.

11

Gran had lunch ready. Anna hardly noticed what she was eating, she was too busy raving about the Wolf Walk.

'To think that this is the same girl I had to drag to the sanctuary last week!' Gran said.

'Not the same,' said Anna. 'I was scared of wolves then.'

'You've obviously been cured of that. Zack can chalk up another convert.'

'Oh, d'you mind if I leave you on your own tonight, Gran? Pete and I are going to see a movie.'

Gran smiled. 'A-a-a-h!'

'I wish you wouldn't do that, Gran.'

'Do what?'

'Say *A-a-a-h!* like you're the all-seeing wise woman.

It's just a movie.'

'Of course it is.'

'It's not like a date or anything.'

'Of course it isn't.'

'We're both at a loose end, we both want to see the movie, so why not see it together?'

'Why not indeed?'

'If you'd rather I stayed in, I can ring Pete and cancel. It's no big deal.'

Gran stood up and began to clear the table. 'Anna, I'm delighted that you and Pete are going to spend some time together,' she said. 'Pete deserves a break from Zack. I don't know how he can stand to live with him – I couldn't.'

'Why don't you and Zack come along? We could make a foursome.'

Gran laughed. 'Some other time, perhaps.'

'Will you be all right while I'm out?'

'There's no need to worry about me, I'm used to being alone. Don't forget your parents are expecting you to call them today. You'd better do it now.'

Anna pulled her mouth down at the corners.

'Don't sulk, it doesn't suit you,' Gran chided.

Anna went to the phone and rang home.

Mum answered. 'Anna! How are you?'

'I'm fine. I went walking with wolves.'

'You did what?'

Anna explained, at length.

Mum didn't seem too taken with the idea. 'Isn't that dangerous?' she said.

'No. The wolves have been humanised and the handlers are specially trained. It was amazing!'

More lengthy explanations, about Zack and the sanctuary.

'You sound happier than when I last spoke to you,' Mum said.

'I am happier. I like it here. How's Dad?'

'Moping. He misses you. He's weeding the garden – shall I fetch him?'

'Don't bother him, but give him my love, will you? I'll ring again on Wednesday.'

'Take care of yourself. Don't get too close to any wolves.'

'Wolves are OK to be close to,' Anna said.

Anna was brushing her hair when Gran shouted, 'Pete's here!'

'I'll be right there.'

Final flick of the brush, check in the wardrobe mirror – she'd do.

Pete was in the kitchen, talking to Gran, nervously jingling a set of ignition keys in his right hand. He was wearing a green hooded fleece that brought out the colour of his eyes. His smile was a reflex action.

'All set?' he said.

'As set as I'll ever be.' Anna kissed Gran goodbye. 'I won't be late.'

'You'll be in by eleven or I shall organise a posse,' Gran threatened. 'Enjoy yourselves.'

Pete drove down the drive, turned on to the main road, then joined the dual carriageway that led to town.

'Is it far?' said Anna.

'Ten more minutes.'

The top of the 2CV was still rolled back; the wind whipped Anna's hair across her face.

'I shouldn't have bothered brushing it!' she said with a laugh.

Pete made no response. He drove the rest of the way in a silence that Anna felt she shouldn't disturb.

The cinema was a multiplex, a glass and neon island in the centre of a car park sea. Pete killed the engine and sat staring straight ahead through the windscreen, both hands gripping the steering wheel.

'There's something I have to tell you,' he said.

'What?'

'This has nothing to do with me. Zack nagged me into asking you out. He worries about my lack of social life.'

Anna remembered the conversation between Zack and Pete at the end of the Wolf Walk – so that was what they'd been talking about. 'Thanks, Pete!' she said. 'You certainly know how to flatter a girl, don't you?'

'I'm telling you because I want to be upfront.'

'Upfront or in my face?'

'I didn't want you to get me wrong.'

'I haven't. Message received and understood. Can we go see the movie now, please?'

They crossed the car park, entered the cinema and joined the queue for tickets.

Pete said, 'My shout, by the way.'

'Uh-uh!'

'Zack gave me the money.'

'Keep it.'

'But—'

'Want me to make a scene, Pete? I'm good at them.'

'I'll bet you are and no, I'd prefer it if you didn't.'

After they'd bought their tickets, Pete said, 'We've got ten minutes before it starts. You want a coke, or popcorn or something?'

'No.'

'I'll let you buy your own.'

Anna started to get angry, then saw that Pete was teasing her, and smiled.

Pete smiled back. 'That's better.'

'What is?'

'You're smiling. You don't smile often enough.'

'Hark who's talking, Mr Intense!'

It didn't go down well; Pete clammed up again.

Inside Studio Four, the signs were ominous. A lot of the audience were thirteen-year-olds who'd come to impress one another; popcorn was flying around the back row.

Pete said, 'Someone ought to sort those kids out.'

'Oh, leave them. Weren't you ever young and foolish?'

'I can't remember.'

The lights dimmed; the back row whistled and jeered. The screen lit up with the words – *This is*

Cinema – just in case anybody was in doubt.

The movie was awful – infantile jokes about parts of the body, and adult-rated swearing. Anna was grateful to the back row for being so noisy, because it drowned out the feeble punch lines.

Forty-five minutes in, Pete leaned over and said, 'Is it me, or does this suck?'

'It sucks,' said Anna. 'Let's get out of here.'

Out in the car park a cool wind was blowing. The sun had gone down but the sky was still blue.

'I don't feel like going back yet,' Anna said. 'Can we grab a coffee someplace?'

'On a Sunday? There's the motorway service station, but I don't want to drive my car on the motorway. I'd get done for slowing.'

'What's slowing?'

'The opposite of speeding.'

They got into the 2CV. Anna fastened her safety belt and said, 'Take me somewhere.'

'Like?'

'Anywhere.'

Pete started the engine. 'You're the boss.'

'No I'm not. I'm Anna and you're Pete – nobody is boss.'

*

Pete drove along winding lanes and took a road that climbed steeply up the side of the hill. At the top of the hill the road levelled out. Pete pulled the car on to a grassy verge and stepped out. Anna followed him along a footpath that stopped at the edge of an almost sheer drop. Below her, the road lights spun themselves into a web.

'Where are we?' she said.

'I don't know if it's got a name. I come here when I need to get away from things.'

'Like Zack?'

'Zack, school – whatever. I like it because it isn't beautiful or ugly. It's kind of…'

'Outstandingly ordinary?' suggested Anna.

Pete's smile gleamed in the fading light. 'There's no pressure here. Where do you go when you're down?'

'The sanctuary.'

'To see Manitou, right? Why are you so keen on him?'

'Because I should be afraid and I'm not. Because he's bigger than I am. Because he treats me like a she wolf and doesn't apologise for it. Like, if you're having a relationship with someone, you analyse everything they say to find out whether they mean it, or you twist their words around until they say what you'd like them to mean. With Manitou, it's just there.'

'Yeah. Wolves are more straightforward than people, aren't they?'

It was too dark for Anna to see Pete's face properly. He could have been anybody, and if he was anybody, it didn't matter what Anna said to him.

'Why don't you like me, Pete?'

'I never said I didn't.'

'But you don't.'

'It's not dislike. It's – when I'm with you, I think—' Pete sighed. 'You frighten me.'

'Why?'

'You're the prickly girl with the great smile. Sometimes I'm curious about what's behind the prickles.'

'Not much. Are you still hurting for Susie?'

Pete wouldn't answer.

'Did she break your heart?' said Anna.

'She did worse than that. She killed my kid.'

'What?'

A gap had appeared in the fence Pete had built around himself, and what he'd been holding back came charging through.

'We were an item for a long time. Things got more and more serious. Then one night…I should've held back but I couldn't. We didn't use anything, you know – take precautions? And, er—' Pete's voice cracked. 'Susie got pregnant. Her dad came to see my dad, told him to keep me away from her. Then my dad had a go at me. It was a total mess, but I thought I could put it right. I figured I could quit school, get a job, get married and support Susie and the baby. I sneaked a message to her and we met in this park. I explained everything to her and she said no. She'd already booked an appointment at a clinic to have an abortion. She didn't want to be lumbered with a kid, and she didn't want to be with me.' Pete laughed. 'Funny, when you discuss abortion in Social Ed, it's – yeah, women have the right to decide what to do with their bodies. But when it's down to you, when it's *your* kid, it isn't so easy to tell what's right.'

'What happened then?'

'I moved in with Zack, partly because Dad was going to Saudi, and partly because everybody in my home town knew. It was like I had to go through it all again every day, and I couldn't stand it. The big joke is that living with Zack made me see that Susie was right.'

'How come?'

'When the cubs were born, they took over. They needed all our time and attention. I thought – if it's like this with wolf cubs, what would having kids be like? If that's what relationships lead to, count me out.'

'Relationships have consequences,' Anna said.

'Damned right, and you don't see the consequences coming until they flatten you.' Pete made a sound like a growl. 'I knew this would happen!'

'What?'

'That I'd tell you. I couldn't tell Zack or Dad, but I had to tell someone. As soon as I saw you, I knew it would be you. I held out long as I could, but tonight… Sorry.'

'For?'

'Like, you really need to listen to my problems.'

'It cuts mine down to size,' Anna said, and she told Pete about Matt. She didn't dress the story up to make herself look hard done by; she told it straight and simple.

It made a link between her and Pete, like the beginning of a friendship.

*

On the drive back to Gran's, Anna said, 'Is something going on between Gran and Zack?'

'Are you kidding? He's crazy about her.'

'Really?'

'Haven't you seen the way he looks at her?'

'But they snap at each other.'

'I don't think much snapping goes on when they're alone together. When Zack takes Jo out for dinner, he's quiet when he comes in. He sticks on the headphones and listens to Beethoven.'

A thought occurred to Anna. 'What do wolves do if an alpha female won't submit to an alpha male?'

'They fight.'

'That's very interesting,' Anna said.

12

Anna didn't see Pete again until Tuesday morning, when she went to work at the sanctuary. Zack gave her a lift, and as they were driving along he said, 'I don't know what you did to my grandson on Sunday, but he's been walking with a new spring in his step ever since.'

'I didn't do anything dramatic,' said Anna. 'He needed to talk and I listened.'

'I was hoping he might. I care for him more than I like to admit, but when it comes to talking – well, the generation gap's too wide, and I'm hardly the person to give advice on matters of the heart.'

'You don't like discussing feelings?'

'What's to discuss? You either have feelings or you don't have them. The rest is just hot air and wasted time. I'd rather get on with my life than talk about it.'

'Come off it, Zack!' Anna said mischievously. 'I've seen you with Manitou. I know that you're a big softie.'

Zack laughed. 'Don't let on to anyone else, will you? They all think I'm an irascible old tyrant.'

'Gran doesn't.'

'Joanna's different. We go back a long way. She helped me through a rough patch after my wife Sarah died. I couldn't have done it without her. She knows me almost as well as you do.'

'Flatterer!'

'There's nothing wrong with flattery, especially when it gets me what I want.'

'And what do you want, Zack?'

'My own way, of course.'

'You and me both! What am I doing today?'

'Checking the stock in the hut, to see what needs to be reordered. But before you do that, someone wants to say hello to you.'

'Who?'

'Manitou. He's restless this morning. He knows you're coming.'

'How could he?'

'Don't ask me,' said Zack. 'I'm only human.'

When Anna stepped out of the pick-up, she heard Manitou barking and yipping. She approached the fence and instead of jumping up, Manitou pressed against the wire, growling softly, his jaws open in a wolf grin.

'Hello, beautiful,' Anna said. 'I've missed you.'

Manitou's eyes looked into hers. The contact was direct and total. Manitou didn't understand his feelings any more than Anna understood hers, but the contact between them was unmistakable and they accepted each other without making demands or setting conditions. Anna felt a huge rush of love.

'Morning!'

Anna turned and saw Pete. 'Hi,' she said.

Pete held out a clipboard. 'Sorry to interrupt, but you'll be needing this.'

'Thanks. You OK?'

'I'm better than OK, but I'm busy right now. Catch you lunchtime?'

'Sure – where?'

'Here with Manitou,' said Pete. 'Where else would you be?'

*

Whoever put the stock away on Sunday had done

a sloppy job, mixing up T-shirts and sweatshirts, jumbling all the sizes together. It took Anna over an hour to sort out the mess. Afterwards she helped Zack to feed the cubs, and took the opportunity to check out the European wolves in the adjoining compound. They were smaller and more wary than the North American wolves, slinking away whenever Anna came near the fence.

'Why are they so shy?' Anna asked Zack.

'I suspect they've had a harder time of it than Manitou and his sisters. We've tried to win their trust, but it hasn't got us very far. Separating the cubs from their mother wasn't pretty. I put her through a lot of distress.'

'Wasn't that cruel?'

'Unforgivably cruel, but it had to be done. People need to be educated about wolves, so the cubs had to be friendly. Hand rearing them was the most efficient way of ensuring that. They've been a great success. They appeal to the public's sentimental side, which is just what I'm after.'

Zack consulted his wristwatch. 'Lunchtime, young lady. Off you go. I'd offer to drive you to Joanna's, but I think Pete might be offended if I did.'

Anna made her way to Manitou's compound. Pete turned up a few minutes later, carrying a plastic bag that contained an apple, a bag of crisps and a can of cola.

'That's your lunch?' said Anna.

'I didn't have a chance to make sandwiches this morning.'

'Want one of mine?'

Pete accepted the offer. 'I've been thinking about you,' he said.

'Is that a good thing or a bad thing?'

'Good, I guess. Sunday night was pretty incredible for me. I don't often open up to someone like that. When Mum died, I shut everybody out. Then Susie got through to me. Then you.'

'You must have been desperate for me to be any use,' Anna said.

'Hey, don't put yourself down, Anna Cope!' Pete took a swig of cola. 'So has Matt been in touch with you since you've been here?'

'No. No one from home has, apart from Mum and Dad. I told my best friend Maggie not to ring me, because I thought Gran might earwig and report back to my parents. I was disappointed that Maggie didn't write to me at first, but now I'm glad. I thought about writing to her, but...that's sort of another life, you know? Like if I tried to explain about the wolves, most of my friends would think I was totally weird.'

'Think you'll get back together with Matt?'

'Maybe,' said Anna.

There'd been a time when she was absolutely certain about her and Matt; now she wasn't so sure.

On Friday evening, Anna wrote in her notebook.

All week I've been thinking about what Pete told me last Sunday, and putting myself in Susie's place. If Dad hadn't come home when he did, maybe Matt and I would have had full-on unprotected sex. I could've got pregnant, and it would've been my fault.

I can't believe how stupid I was. As soon as Matt and I started getting physical, I should have gone to a contraceptive clinic, but I didn't. I was scared that Mum and Dad would find out, scared I might be asked embarrassing questions. Most of all, it wouldn't have fitted with what I thought was romantic, Matt and I weren't about all those bits of rubber, and pills, and plastic and wire things.

Would I have had an abortion, like Susie? Could I have lived with that? I don't think that abortion is murder, but any way you look at it, it's the ending of a life. An embryo might not be a person, but it isn't a thing.

And if I'd decided to keep the baby – what's pregnancy like? I know about the morning sickness and craving for weird food, because those are the parts you see on TV and in movies. What about the parts they don't show? Everybody says that giving birth is painful, but how painful? What kind of pain? Where does it hurt? Could I stand it if I had one of those complicated deliveries that goes on for hours and hours?

Then there'd be the baby, feeding it, dressing it, changing nappies. Babies have a soft point on their skulls, and if you press it too hard they die. How d'you keep them protected?

With a baby to take care of, I couldn't go out anywhere, I couldn't afford to do anything. And would Matt be there? I try to imagine him being a father – leaving for work at eight, coming home at six, patting the baby on the back when it needs burping – but I can't. Matt hasn't finished being a boy yet, and I haven't finished being a girl. Anyway, look at Gran. Her marriage broke up after twenty years. How long would Matt and I last?

I want all that one day – a partner (not necessarily a husband), kids – but I don't want it now. I don't want *to bring a child into the world and resent it for ruining my life.*

Consequences.

I've been to the sanctuary most days, sometimes for a couple of hours, sometimes longer. I've been promoted. I get to scrub out the dens as well as doing the other things I do. Yesterday I fed the cubs – second time this week – and played with them. While I was playing with Loki, Manitou was watching me. Do wolves get jealous? I wish I could have played with him when he was a cub. I think he wishes the same thing.

Never thought I'd say this, but Pete and I are matey. Now we know our BIG SECRETS, we've started telling each other a lot of other stuff as well. He's not a jerk. He's warm and funny, like Zack but without the crabbiness. We take the mick out of each other. Pete's helping me. Hope I'm helping him.

How much did Zack and Gran have to do with this? Were they like – stick two miserable teenagers together, see if they form a therapy group?

I could ask Gran, I suppose, but I'd rather think that Pete and I were the right people in the right place at the right time – like it was fate.

Leave me some illusions, please!

*

The letter arrived the following morning. Anna found it on the work surface in the kitchen.

Gran was standing over the stove, boiling eggs. 'Post for you,' she said.

'So I see.'

'Girl's handwriting, by the look of the envelope.'

It seemed an odd remark, until Anna worked it out. 'It's not Matt's writing, Gran.'

'I didn't think so.'

'Did Mum and Dad ask you to keep an eye on my mail?'

'Yes.'

'Would you have given me the letter if you thought it was from Matt?'

'I'm relieved not to be in a position where I have to answer that. I told you, I'm not on anyone's side.'

'That's a cop-out!'

'It most certainly is. Take a seat, the eggs are ready.'

After breakfast, Anna read the letter in her room. It was from Maggie.

Dear Anna,

This is a tough letter for me to write and it's going to be even tougher for you to read, so I'm going to get it over with as fast as I can.

Matt's going out with Jane Fuller.

I found out from Liz Parker. She told me she'd seen Matt snogging Jane outside some club. I thought Liz must have got things wrong, so I went to see Matt.

It's true, Anna. Sorry. Matt says he can't go on after what happened, that it would be better to make a clean break, put the past behind him and blah-blah. It was a load of crap. The guy is a sleazebag. You're worth way more than him. When you come back, boys will be lining up to ask you out, you wait and see.

Talking of which - Jonathan

Field stopped me in the street on Wednesday morning. You remember Jonathan, Mr Dream Buns?

He said, 'Is it right what I hear about Matt and Jane being an item?'

I said, 'I wouldn't know. I never listen to gossip.' (TEE HEE!)

He said, 'Is Anna with anyone?'

I said, 'She's at her Gran's. I've got no idea what she's up to.'

I mean, was that I AM INTERESTED, or what?

I know you'll be upset about Matt. When Phil finished with me, I was - that's it, my life is over! But it didn't last for long. I'm over it now. Just the occasional twinge. You'll get over it too.

If you want to talk, you know the number. If you want to write, that's OK too.

Take care, see ya,
Maggie

Anna went downstairs, where Gran was hovering.

Anna said, 'Tell Mum and Dad they can relax. Matt dumped me.'

'Anna, I—'

Anna held up her hand. 'Spare me, Gran. I'm fine.'

'I'm here if you need me.'

'I know, and thanks. I have to let it sink in.'

Anna's mind was saying, Avoid! Delay! Put it off! Think about something else!

Saturday afternoon, Anna was split in two. Half of her was at the sanctuary with Pete, setting up the tables outside the hut; the other half was at the world première of *Anna and Matt*, a docu-soap that included their first date, first kiss, all the places they'd been together, everything they'd said and done.

It was *Jane and Matt* now. Matt was Jane's. He didn't belong to Anna any more.

Did he ever? Anna thought. Does anyone ever belong to anyone else? You can't own people, you just borrow them until they get bored, or things get too complicated. We went too far, too fast.

The visitors arrived, high on contact with the wolves. Anna threw herself into making drinks and giving change, but when the visitors had gone the memories closed in again.

As they were folding the trestles of the big table, Pete said, 'Spill.'

'Huh?'

'You've had a black halo round your head all afternoon.'

There was no getting past Pete.

Anna said, 'The love of my life has found someone else he likes better than me. My friend Maggie wrote and told me. I got the letter this morning.'

'No!'

'Yes, and please don't say how sorry you are. I can be sorry for myself.'

'Don't be. You're better off without him.'

'How d'you make that out?'

'If he prefers another girl to you, he's an idiot.'

'Excuse me,' said Anna, 'was there a compliment in there somewhere?'

Pete stopped doing what he was doing and made eye contact. 'I mean it. If he's chucked you, it's his loss.'

'Cut it out, Pete. My ego doesn't need boosting.'

'Oh, yes it does! Once you start wallowing, it's hard

to stop. It can get so's you enjoy it.'

'Hey?'

Pete struck a melodramatic pose, the back of his left hand pressed to his forehead. 'Oh, the pain! Oh, the heartache! Everybody gather around and watch me bleed!' He let his hand drop. 'Believe me, I was the same way myself for a while.'

'What made you stop?'

'I met this girl called Anna. She beat it out of me with sarcasm.'

'And how d'you feel now?'

'Bruised, but not crippled. How about you?'

Anna struggled for the right words. 'I can't tell. I ought to be angry but…if Matt and I had got back together, we would've had to keep it a secret from my parents. That would've meant lying, snatching time together, being afraid. It would've felt wrong.'

'And when it feels wrong, it *is* wrong.'

'I guess.'

'So has Matt let you down, or off the hook?'

It was a very good question.

Anna said, 'Wouldn't it be great if you could take a break from being human and be something else.'

'What would you be?'

'A she wolf. I'd join Manitou in the compound and I wouldn't have to think about anything. I'd be free.'

'Except for the fence,' said Pete.

13

Next morning at breakfast, Gran produced a mound of pancakes dripping with melted butter, maple syrup and lemon juice, a jug of freshly-ground coffee; there was even a small vase of sweet peas in the middle of the dining table.

'What are we celebrating?' Anna asked.

'I thought you could do with pampering.'

'Are you trying to build up my self-esteem?'

'What's wrong with that?'

'I'm not complaining.'

Anna ate so many pancakes that she was ashamed of herself.

'Your appetite has returned, I see,' said Gran. 'That's a good sign.'

'It is?'

'Yes. It means you're taking care of yourself. It's all very romantic to pine away for love, but there's no point in moping over what can't be changed. Count your blessings.'

'And they would be?'

'You're young, bright, pretty and the world is full of possibilities. We all make mistakes, the trick is to admit them and move on.'

Anna wondered if she'd already moved on. If she hadn't been caught out, she would have missed a lot – getting to know Gran as an equal, meeting Zack, Pete and Manitou. She'd still be Dumb Anna, drooling over designer labels, listening to the latest goss, putting Matt through hoops so that she could use him to explore herself. The Anna she was now wouldn't exist.

The phone rang.

Gran sighed irritatedly and stood up. 'Who's that disturbing my day of rest?'

Gran was on the phone for a long time. Anna heard her talking in the quietly exasperated voice people used when they were having an argument that they didn't want overheard.

'What? You're being completely unreasonable,

Zack, it might not be convenient for me to… You can't expect me to just drop everything and… Very well, but it depends on…I'll see.'

Gran raised her voice. 'Anna? Pete would like to talk to you.'

Pete said, 'How you doing?'

'I'm good,' said Anna. 'You?'

'Zack's on my case. He wants me out of the way this afternoon. I'm going for a walk. Want to come along?'

'Sure.'

'I'll pick you up after lunch. Two o'clock do you?'

'Yup. See you then.'

Anna put down the phone. 'I'm going out with Pete this afternoon,' she told Gran.

'Hmm?'

'I'm going out with Pete this afternoon. Is that OK?'

'Why shouldn't it be?'

'You might have something planned.'

'No, not really.'

Gran wasn't with it; she was someplace inside herself where she didn't want to be.

Anna said, 'Was that Zack you were talking to before?'

'Hmm?'

'Are you feeling all right, Gran?'

'Yes. I'm a little preoccupied at the moment – nothing you need concern yourself with.'

Which was Gran's way of telling Anna to butt out.

Pete and Anna left the 2CV at the side of the road and turned left into a lane that had a hawthorn hedge on either side. The lane was locked by a rustic five-bar gate that looked like an obstacle in a show-jumping ring. Pete climbed on to the gate and straddled it.

'Should we be doing this?' said Anna. 'The sign says it's council property.'

'It's cool. We've got permission. This is another place where we walk the wolves.'

Pete held out his hand to help Anna up; Anna reached out, then pulled her hand away. 'I don't need any help, thanks,' she said.

On the far side of the fence, the lane dwindled to a footpath that ran between fir trees. The trees had red bark, studded with beads of hardened resin that glinted like sweat; the ground was carpeted with dried needles.

'How come Zack booted you out?' Anna said.

'Search me. When I asked him, he told me it was

none of my business. He was in a tetchy mood this morning.'

'Gran was acting weird too. Have they had a row?'

'Not that I know of.'

The path descended a slope to a black pool that smelled stagnant. A cloud of midges danced in front of Anna's face and she tried to swat them away.

'Pipe smoke gets rid of them,' Pete said.

'Aw, shucks! I didn't think to bring my pipe with me. I didn't realise I was going to be eaten to death.'

They came to a muddy trickle that fed the pool. Branches had been set into the mud to form a crude bridge. Pete slipped on the branches and only just managed to keep his balance.

'Grab my hand, I'll pull you across,' he said.

'I don't want to be pulled.'

'You don't want to be covered in mud either.'

Reluctantly, Anna took Pete's hand; just like she'd feared, his touch gave her a tingle that went on after she'd let his hand go.

The trees pressed in closer, casting a communal shadow that was pierced by shafts of dusty light. Pete sat down on a fallen trunk that was worn as smooth as bone. Anna sat next to him.

'How's the heartache?' said Pete.

'Not so bad.'

'Didn't cry yourself to sleep then?'

'No.'

'You're lucky. You heal fast.'

'Maybe I wasn't wounded in the first place. It's like you said, I was starting to enjoy wallowing, you know? Drama queens have the best lines because they write their own scripts.'

'Tell me about it.'

'Pete, you know that feeling you get when someone you care about cares about you?'

'Yes.'

'Does it ever come back, or does it only happen once?'

Anna's eyes met Pete's; the air went still.

Pete said, 'It would be really easy for us to get involved, wouldn't it?'

'Yes.'

'That's what scares me about you. I want to kiss you.'

'I know.'

'But it isn't going to happen, is it?'

'No.'

'Because you don't want to?'

'No, because I *do* want to,' Anna said. 'If we kiss, it all changes. We have to do the girl-boy thing.'

'Jealousy, misunderstanding, arguing about stupid stuff, breaking up and getting back together—'

'Who needs it? This is better. I can say what I want to you.'

'Me too.'

'I don't want to chuck it away for a quick snog and a grope.'

Pete burst out laughing. 'You're just a sentimental fool, aren't you?' he said.

Anna leaned over and kissed the end of his nose.

Pete said, 'You're a special person, Anna Cope. I'm glad you're here.'

Just before the 2CV reached the turn-off for Gran's, Zack's pick-up truck came barrelling out of the entrance, on to the main road. The truck swerved over the central white line, straightened up and screeched away in a blue mist of vaporised tyre rubber.

Pete said, 'What the—'

'Pull over!' said Anna. 'Something's up. You go after Zack, I'll check on Gran.'

Pete stopped the car. Anna clambered out and hurried up the drive, fumbling in her pocket for the front door key. Her hands were clumsy; she forgot which way the lock turned.

Gran was on the sofa, dabbing at her red, puffy eyes with a tissue.

'Gran?'

'Oh, dear! You pick your moments, don't you, Anna?'

'What's the matter?'

Gran attempted a brave smile, but it wobbled too much for her to hold. 'It's nothing.'

Anna plonked herself down on the sofa and put her arm around Gran's shoulders. 'Don't give me that!' she said. 'Tell me or I'll wheedle it out of you.'

'This is ridiculous. I'm behaving like an adolescent.'

'Thanks a bunch.'

Gran took a shuddery breath. 'It's Zack,' she said.

'I know it's Zack. Pete and I nearly collided with him just now. What about Zack?'

'You'll probably find it hard to believe this of somebody my age, but over the last eighteen months Zack and I have been having what used to be called an affair.'

'It's not hard to believe. Stop apologising and cut to the chase.'

'It was mutually convenient when it began. We were two old friends, sharing our loneliness. Occasionally Zack would stay the night here, or I'd stay at his place – not so much since Pete came on the scene, of course. It was a civilised arrangement – no pressure, no urgency. It was there when we both felt like it.'

'But?'

'It's not enough for Zack. He wants to marry me.'

'That's great, Gran!'

'No it isn't! How could I possibly marry again? I can't give up my independence and share my life with someone else. I'm too old and Zack's too domineering. It would mean my making compromises that I'm not prepared to make.'

'D'you love him?'

The directness of the question flustered Gran. 'I'm very fond of him,' she said evasively.

'Stop wriggling, Gran! D'you love the guy or not?'

'I love him when he keeps his distance, when I can walk away from him, close the door and sleep alone in my own bed.'

'Are you frightened of commitment?'

Gran's eyebrows shot up. 'I'm the one who makes sage pronouncements, thank you. Me pensioner, you teenager – remember?'

'What will you do?'

'Allow Zack a suitable cooling-off period, then rebuild bridges.'

'Don't leave it too long, Gran,' Anna advised.

Gran went to bed at ten. Anna waited fifteen minutes before she rang Zack's number, hoping that Pete would answer; her luck was in.

'How's Zack?' Anna asked.

'Hitting the scotch. How's Jo?'

'Confused.'

'You know he proposed and she turned him down?'

'Yeah. I reckon she's being pig-headed. Maybe we should sit them down and talk some sense into them.'

'Maybe not. Let them sort themselves out. It isn't the first time that this has happened.'

'Isn't it?'

'Zack proposes to Jo every three months or so. He thinks he can wear her down.'

'He'd better do it soon, or they'll be going up the aisle in wheelchairs.'

'It's their lives. I say we leave them to it.'

Pete was right; watching Gran and Zack was like making a wildlife documentary – the first rule was no interference.

14

The next morning Anna sat on the edge of her bed and made an entry in her notebook.

I just read through all this stuff I've been writing. It started out as a long letter to Matt but it's changed into a letter to me. I've been writing to myself. Is that a sign of madness, like talking to yourself?

Plenty of crazy thoughts are going through my head right now.

Did I do it on purpose? When I went in the bedroom with Matt, I knew I was taking a big risk, but did I deliberately set it up so that we'd get caught? Maybe somewhere in the back of my mind I knew that the relationship wasn't going anywhere and wasn't good for us, so I kind of arranged a wham bam ending where I could dump all the blame on Mum and Dad – true lovers torn apart by wicked parents sort of thing.

I don't know – does fate happen to you, or do you make it happen?

And now there's Pete. How do I untangle that lot? Every time I try to put a label on our relationship, it won't stick.

Friendship? Yeah, up to a point. We've got really close, really quickly, and I've never had a boy as a close friend before, so I don't know how it's supposed to work. I didn't even know that a boy and a girl could *be close friends.*

Love? Not the kind that Matt and I had. Sure, I can fantasise about me and Pete getting it together, holding hands in the moonlight, kissing, getting horny – but I don't want to do anything about it. It has to stay a fantasy because if I tried to make it real I'd get sucked back into how I was with Matt.

Which leaves? The way it is. It doesn't have to be anything else. It's a holiday romance without the romance.

This is dead corny, but I'm going to put it anyway.

I keep getting a memory flash from some TV programme I watched about eagles. They'd built a nest way up on a ledge, and these two fledglings were learning about flying. They perched on the edge of the nest, opened their wings, and the wind lifted them up a few centimetres and dropped them down again. The fledglings were spooked, like they knew they'd fly eventually, but they weren't ready yet.

Pete and I are like that. One day we'll go over the edge and fly, but for the moment we're still trying out our wings.

Cutesy, huh? Two eagles soaring into the sunset to the sound of violins while THE END rolls up on the screen.

Mrs Joanna Hebron. That doesn't look so bad. Why is Gran scared of it? It's nice to think of her and Zack together, taking care of each other, getting wrinklier and more crotchety. I'd get to call Zack Grandad – that would rattle his cage!

On the other hand, why isn't Zack happy with the way things are between him and Gran? Sounds ideal to me.

When whoever-it-is comes along, I'm going to—

Nah! Who am I kidding? I'll improvise, the same as everyone else. You can't predict what's going to happen in a relationship, any more than you can predict the future. It's not so much getting things right, as knowing how not to get them wrong. You build on failure. That's what I'm—

There was a knock on the bedroom door. Anna put

down her pen and closed the notebook.

'Come in.'

Gran pushed open the door; she was shaking. 'Pete's just been on the phone,' she said. 'He wanted to know if Zack was here.'

'Zack?'

Gran nodded. 'Zack went out with Manitou at six o'clock this morning. Pete hasn't seen him since.'

Anna looked at her watch. It was five past nine.

Gran said, 'I'm going to drive over to the sanctuary.'

Anna stood up. 'I'll come with you. Let's get going.'

On the way to Zack's, Gran lost it. She crashed the gears and didn't use her indicators. Angry drivers flashed their headlights at her.

'Take it easy, Gran,' Anna said.

'How can I, after what I said to Zack yesterday? He was in such a rage when he left. If he's had an accident, I'll never forgive myself.'

'Getting us killed in a car smash isn't going to help, Gran.'

Gran slowed down and tried to get a grip. 'I'm concerned because Zack had a mild heart attack three years ago. A specialist warned him to avoid stress, but Zack was too cussed to pay any attention.'

They came up behind a tractor. Gran crawled along for a hundred metres, then leaned on the horn, rolled down her window and yelled, 'Get out of the bloody way!'

'Gran?' said Anna. 'Don't you have a mild heart attack. Get us there in one piece, OK?'

Pete was outside the compound, pacing like the she wolves. He looked on the verge of tears, or throwing up, or both. He walked over to the car and started to babble.

'I don't know what to do. I'm here on my own. The volunteers aren't due till ten. I couldn't leave the wolves. I've tried Zack's mobile, but he must have switched it off.'

Dealing with Pete helped Gran to deal with herself. 'I'll stay here and hold the fort, you and Anna go and look for Zack,' she said. 'Take my mobile with you, Anna. It's in my handbag on the back seat. Have the wolves been fed, Pete?'

'Not yet.'

'I'll see to them. Phone me as soon as you have any news. I'll phone you if he turns up here.' Gran gave Pete's arm a squeeze. 'He's probably sulking somewhere, you know what he's like. When you find him, tell him

I'm going to kill him the next time I see him.'

Anna grabbed Gran's mobile and followed Pete to the 2CV. Pete started the engine and drove up the drive.

'Where do we start?' said Anna.

'That place we went yesterday. If we don't find him, we try Hencham Wood.'

'And if he's not there?'

'Then he could be anywhere. Most likely in a pub car park, waiting for opening time.'

'Would he do that when he's got Manitou with him?'

'After the mood he was in last night, Zack's liable to do anything.'

Pete gave way for a lorry at a mini roundabout; he didn't drive on after the lorry had passed by.

'What am I going to do if something's happened to him, Anna? He's practically all I've got. I've never told him how much he means to me.'

Anna wasn't feeling calm or sensible, but she knew that Pete needed to think she was. 'There's no time for this, Pete,' she said. 'Focus on finding Zack.'

Pete sniffed, said, 'You're right,' and got the car moving again.

They found Zack's truck and trailer on the same stretch of road where they'd parked the day before. Both the truck and the trailer were empty.

'He's around here someplace,' said Pete. 'You go the same way we went yesterday, I'll start from the other end of the trail.'

'No. We should stick together.'

If Zack was dead, Anna didn't want to discover the body on her own; neither did Pete.

This time the wood was a bad dream: there were faces in the trunks of the trees; the gloom was sinister. It reminded Anna of an illustration in a book she'd been given when she was a kid – *Grimm's Fairy Tales*. There were spirits in the shadows, ready to entice little girls off the path and into the dark.

'Zack?' Pete shouted. 'Zack!'

His voice didn't carry; the trees deadened its sound.

Anna listened: bird song; wind hissing through the pines.

They dropped down the slope towards the stagnant pool. Every so often Anna saw paw prints, the pattern from the sole of a boot.

'Zack!'

Anna wished that Pete would stop shouting; it

made her want to join in and she wasn't sure if she'd be able to keep her shout from turning into a wail.

Pete stood still and pointed. 'What's that?'

Anna gazed in the direction of Pete's outstretched finger.

Someone had left a bundle of muddy clothes beside the stream – jacket, jumper, jeans, a pair of old boots.

Then Anna realised that the bundle was Zack and she started to run.

Zack had fallen on the greasy branches that crossed the stream. He lay on his side with his eyes closed, his left foot twisted out at an impossible angle. His face was white, his nose and lips were blue. There was a gash in his temple; the blood had run into his hair and dried black.

Pete and Anna crouched down.

'Zack?' said Pete.

Zack's eyelids fluttered open and he grunted. 'Well it's about bloody time!'

'Are you hurt?'

'No, I'm lying in the mud because I was told it's good for the complexion. Left ankle's broken. I heard it snap.'

Anna handed the mobile to Pete. 'Phone Gran,' she

said. 'Tell her to call an ambulance.'

'Joanna knows?' said Zack. 'God, I'll never hear the end of it!'

Pete pressed buttons; swore. 'It's not working. I can't get through.'

'The trees must be interfering,' said Anna. 'Try from the top of the ridge. I'll stay with Zack.'

The only bit of First Aid that Anna knew was that accident victims had to be kept warm, so she took off her jacket and placed it over Zack's chest; it was too small to be of much use.

Zack said, 'I'm an idiot. I knew I was too old to handle him properly any more, but I wouldn't admit it to myself. Had to play the he man, didn't I?'

'Are you in pain?'

'Can't feel a thing yet. That'll be shock. Keep your fingers crossed that the ambulance gets here before it wears off.' Zack's voice went squeaky, like an old man's. 'And I've wet my trousers.'

'Don't worry about it.'

'Broken ankle, incontinent – not much bloody use, am I? What time is it?'

'Ten past ten.'

'That late? I must have passed out. It's true what

they say, there's no fool like an old fool.'

Anna knew that something else was wrong and looked around to place it. She noticed a long chain fastened to Zack's right wrist by a leather strap. The far end of the chain lay in an empty loop; there were tawny hairs caught between the links.

'Zack, where's Manitou?'

Zack laughed, then gasped. 'Felt that one!' he said through clenched teeth. 'Only hurts when I laugh, so don't tell me any jokes.'

'Where's Manitou?'

'Gone. He was too strong for me. I slipped and he yanked me head over heels. A branch got caught under the choke chain. Took him ten minutes to figure out how to slip it. Smart wolf. Damned sight smarter than I am.'

'But where's he gone?'

'Wherever his fancy takes him. A wolf's preferred means of locomotion is a trot. He can keep up a speed of between twelve and eighteen kilometres an hour all day. I left the sanctuary at six. Drive lasted twenty minutes. Half an hour's walk to get here. Manitou must have got loose about seven. He could be fifty kilometres away by now.'

'But he'll head for the sanctuary, won't he?'

'If he's got any sense, but who can tell? He's scenting all kinds of things for the first time. He'll be excited – no chain pulling at him, no human to hold him back. He might find a lair and mark out a new territory.'

'He wouldn't attack anybody, would he? Like if he got cornered?'

Zack snorted in disgust. 'Good God, girl, haven't you learned anything about wolves? He'll give people a wide berth. That's not my main concern.'

'What is?'

'Manitou will leave people alone, but will they leave him alone?'

Pete came clumping down the path. 'The ambulance is on its way,' he panted.

'Have you rung the police?' Zack demanded.

'Not yet. I thought—'

'Call them right away, and the local council.'

Anna didn't understand. 'Why the police?'

'The law classifies wolves as dangerous animals,' Zack said. 'The police have to be contacted as soon as one escapes.'

'What will the police do?'

A second spasm of pain made Zack suck air.

It was Pete who answered Anna's question. 'They'll notify all the farms in the area,' he said, 'and they'll send marksmen after Manitou.'

15

The ambulance arrived. Two medics carried a stretcher down to Zack and gave him a shot of sedative before they lifted him on to it.

While he was waiting for the drug to take effect, Zack barked out last-minute instructions to Pete.

'Wait for the police. Make sure they get their facts straight.'

'I was going to come to the hospital with you.'

'I don't want you hovering at my bedside. The doctors and nurses will take care of me – that's what they're paid for. You've got more important things to do.'

'Yes, Zack.'

'Give George a call. He's up to speed on the admin that needs doing.'

'Yes, Zack.'

'And get in touch with those advertising people.'

'Yes, Zack.'

'And…' the tension went out of Zack's face as his eyes started to glaze over, '…find Manitou before the police do, Pete. Think wolf.'

'I'll try my best, Zack.'

Zack didn't hear; he was asleep.

Five minutes after the ambulance left, a police car pulled up behind Zack's truck and two constables got out. One was tall and bulky, the other was shorter, with watery-grey eyes that didn't blink. The short policeman asked all the questions; the tall one took notes.

'Is your name Peter Hebron?'

'Yes.'

'You rang in to report the escape of a dangerous animal?'

'Yes.'

'Can you give us a description of the animal?'

'A fully-grown male North American grey wolf, one point eight metres long, standing seventy-five centimetres high at the shoulder, weighing a hundred and fifty kilos.'

The tall policeman whistled.

The short policeman said, 'You seem very definite about the details.'

'Manitou is weighed and measured regularly.'

'Manitou?'

'The wolf answers to the name of Manitou.'

'Have you any idea as to the likely whereabouts of this...Manitou?'

'If I did, I wouldn't be standing here talking to you.'

'And who is responsible for keeping the wolf?'

'My grandfather, Zachariah Hebron. He's director of the wolf sanctuary at—'

'That's all right, son,' said the tall policeman. 'We know where the wolf sanctuary is.' He lowered his voice to talk to his companion. 'Better get some back-up.'

Anna saw the look that passed between the two men. 'Please, if you find Manitou, don't shoot him,' she said. 'Call the sanctuary. They'll send a trained handler to collect him. Manitou won't hurt anybody.'

The short policeman turned to Anna; he spoke like a machine. 'Rest assured that our officers in the field will do all they can to ensure the welfare of the animal, miss. They'll use their best judgement to appraise the situation and take such action as they deem appropriate.'

Pete said, 'Let me join the search. Manitou knows me. He might come to me. You won't need to use guns.'

'My advice to you is to return home and stay by your telephone, sir. You'll be contacted as soon as there are any developments. These matters are best handled by experienced personnel.'

'Yeah?' said Pete. 'How much experience of hunting wolves have you had, Constable?'

The expression on the policeman's face said that Pete was pushing his luck.

The policemen drove off, and Anna and Pete spent the next hour searching the wood. They tracked Manitou as far as the road, then the trail ran out.

'This is hopeless,' said Pete. 'I should get back to the sanctuary. I'll drop you off on the way.'

'I'd rather stay with you.'

Pete shook his head. 'I need some time on my own. I can't think straight at the moment. D'you mind?'

'Yes, but I'll live. Ring me if there's anything I can do.'

'You've already done loads.'

'Promise!'

'OK, OK, I promise – happy?' Pete snapped. His shoulders sagged. 'I'm sorry, Anna. I didn't mean to bite your head off. I'm worried about Zack and I'm worried about Manitou.'

Anna wanted to give Pete a hug, but she was afraid that he might push her away.

Back at Gran's, Anna found a red light winking on the answerphone; she pressed *play*.

Gran's voice said, 'It's me, Anna. I'm at the sanctuary, it's twelve o'clock and I'm just about to leave for the hospital to see Zack. I probably won't be back until this evening. It's chaos here. The media have got hold of the story and the phone hasn't stopped ringing. I'll catch you later. Make sure you eat something.'

Anna made herself a salad sandwich, which she ate without tasting, then went up to her room and sat staring at Gran's drawing of Manitou.

Don't stay out there, she thought. Go to the sanctuary where it's safe. Be there the next time I visit. Jump up on the fence when you see me. You matter to me. I want to know all there is to know about you, and I can't do it if you're not there.

Anna closed her eyes. She felt helpless; thinking wasn't going to achieve anything, but how could she stop herself from doing it?

Manitou got a mention in the national TV news at six o'clock; the regional news programme ran the story as its main feature. They treated it as a comedy, starting off with a wolf howl dubbed on to a recording of *The Teddy Bears' Picnic*.

The presenter said, 'And if the residents of West Berkshire go down to the woods this evening, they may be in for a very big surprise indeed. A wolf has broken out of a sanctuary near Newbury, and farmers are concerned about the threat it may pose to them. We sent our intrepid reporter, Bob Cadbury, to investigate.'

More wolf howls; old documentary footage of a pack of Canadian wolves tearing chunks out of a dead caribou. The voice-over used words like, 'killer', 'ruthless predator', and 'ancient enemy'. There were no facts in the commentary, it was all folklore.

The reporter interviewed a farmer. The farmer wore a waxed-cotton coat and cradled a shotgun in the crook of his left arm.

'This is Frank Weston, who owns a dairy farm in the neighbourhood of the wolf sanctuary. Tell me, Mr Weston, how do you feel about a wolf being loose in the area?'

'Unhappy, obviously,' the farmer said. 'When I think of the damage a wolf could do to my herd – well.'

'Did you know about the sanctuary?'

'Oh yes. I've written more than a dozen letters to the authorities, complaining about it. No one should be allowed to keep wolves near a farm, stands to reason.'

'And how did the authorities react?'

'With a lot of jargon about their inspectors reporting that the security arrangements were satisfactory.' The farmer laughed scornfully. 'I don't call it satisfactory to have a wild animal running free, and nor does any farmer I know of.'

'What extra precautions will you be taking tonight?'

The farmer hefted the shotgun. 'I'm going walking in the fields and I'm taking this with me,' he said. 'If I catch that wolf, I'll give him both barrels.'

The reporter smiled into the camera. 'This is Bob Cadbury in West Berkshire, returning you to the studio.'

Anna's heart sank. There was no balance in the report, no one gave the wolves' side; the fairy-tale bogeyman made more entertaining TV.

Pete rang a few minutes later. 'Did you see the news?' he said.

'Yes. It was horrible.'

'Tomorrow the place is going to be crawling with armed nutters, out to bag a wolf.'

'I'm scared, Pete.'

'Keep it together. I may have got it cracked. I reckon Manitou will head for Staynor Park. It's about forty kilometres from here.'

'Why would he go there?'

'They keep deer, and that's wild wolves' primary food source. If he gets the scent, he'll track them down.'

'You've been thinking wolf,' Anna said admiringly.

'I've been using logic. Wolves don't like to hunt at night, so my guess is that he'll wait until morning. I'm going to check it out first thing tomorrow.'

'It's a bit if, but and maybe, isn't it?'

'Got a better plan?'

'No.'

'Are you going to come with me?'

'You want me to?'

'It'll be easier to get him on a lead if there's two of us.

If you want to help, I'll pick you up at the end of Jo's drive at four.'

'In the *morning*?'

'Wolves are early risers.'

'I'll be there.'

Gran came home just after seven, looking shattered. She flopped on the sofa, kicked off her shoes and wriggled her toes. 'I hate hospitals!' she grumbled. 'All that hanging about.'

'How's Zack?'

'In his element – lots of young nurses to order around. He's got them eating out of his hand.'

'How are you?'

'Relieved and angry. I could strangle the old goat. I hurt his male pride, so next day he takes Manitou out on his own to prove to himself how macho he is.'

'He's going to be OK though?'

'Eventually. He'll have to wear a plaster and that's going to make him even more insufferable. How are you bearing up?'

'I'm fine.'

'You don't look fine. You look like Zack. He's frantic about Manitou. According to him, the police are a bunch of trigger-happy lunatics.'

'What if he's right, Gran?'

Gran gave Anna a searching look. 'Try not to fret, love. I know how you feel, I'm anxious myself.'

'I can't help it, Gran.'

'All we can do is carry on, and wait.'

Anna considered telling Gran about Staynor Park, but if she did there was no way that Gran would allow her to go jaunting off at four in the morning to hunt for a wolf that not even Zack could handle.

Gran said, 'I should shake my bones and start dinner. Have you eaten?'

'I hung on for you.'

'Pasta and garlic bread?'

'I'll get it, you take it easy.'

'We'll both get it. It'll give us something else to think about.'

They went into the kitchen. Gran lit the oven for the garlic bread. 'I hope I'm not sticking my nose in where it's not wanted, Anna,' she said, 'but I couldn't help noticing that you and Pete seem to be rubbing along rather well these days.'

'We don't do any rubbing. It's not that sort of relationship.'

'You know what I mean.'

'We like each other. We're friends.'

'Really?'

'Really. Just friends. Give me a break, will you, Gran? What Matt and I got up to was dumb and I'm not about to try it again. I'm not eating my heart out for him. I'm over it.'

And though Anna hadn't known it until she said it, it was true. Compared with her fears for Manitou, the whole business with Matt was pathetic.

16

The note said:

GRAN,

PETE THINKS HE KNOWS WHERE
MANITOU IS. WE'RE GOING TO FIND HIM. I HOPE
YOU'RE NOT MAD AT ME. IF YOU ARE, YOU CAN
GROUND ME FOR THE REST OF THE HOLIDAY. I
WANTED TO TELL YOU, BUT YOU WOULD HAVE
TRIED TO STOP ME AND I HAVE TO DO THIS.
LOTS OF LOVE,
ANNA.

Anna put the note on the dining table and left the
house as quietly as possible.

It was cold. In the clear sky, the stars wavered as if

they were underwater. Anna walked down the driveway and waited at the side of the road, hugging herself to keep warm. Her eyes felt gritty from lack of sleep.

'Get a move on, Pete!' she muttered. 'I'm so cold, my bum's about to drop off.'

A pair of headlights flashed over the brow of a hill. Anna followed the headlights as they drew closer.

It was Pete, driving Zack's truck and trailer. He stopped the truck and leaned across the cab to open the door for Anna. Anna got in; warmth from the truck's heater washed over her.

Pete put the truck in gear and drove on. 'It shouldn't take us long,' he said. 'There's hardly any traffic about.'

'That doesn't surprise me. Only people who aren't in their right minds are on the road this early. What's the plan? Are we going to knock on the front door and ask for our wolf back?'

'I've brought a torch and a lead. We'll scout around for signs of Manitou. If we spot any, we go in after him, find him, put him on the lead and get out fast.'

'Have you ever put Manitou on a lead?' asked Anna.

'No.'

'Can you do it?'

'As long as he lets me,' Pete said.

Anna didn't want to think about what might happen if Manitou didn't cooperate, so she talked about something else. 'Gran tells me that Zack's doing OK.'

'He's indestructible. He'll need to be.'

'Oh?'

'He's going to be facing a charge of gross negligence. He'll get a hefty fine and lose his licence to keep dangerous animals.'

Anna frowned. 'Will the sanctuary be closed down?' she said.

'Possibly. It depends on how good a lawyer we can get. If we stay open, somebody else will have to take over.'

'Like who?'

'George,' said Pete. 'He's Zack's partner and he's got a licence too. If Zack pleads guilty, admits to acting irresponsibly and grovels, we might swing it.'

'That doesn't sound like Zack to me.'

'He'll do what's best for the wolves.' Pete stifled a yawn. 'At the moment, it isn't Zack's future that bothers me, it's the police. If I can connect Manitou to

Staynor Park, so can they. They might have the place staked out. We could get ourselves arrested for trespassing, if we're not careful.'

'Then we'll be careful,' Anna said.

They passed a brown and white sign – *Staynor House and Deer Park.*

Between the hedges and trees at the side of the road, Anna caught glimpses of a large building in the distance.

Pete turned down a lane and parked the truck close to a shallow ditch. On the opposite side of the lane was another ditch and a low bank. Wooden fencing had been fixed to uprights sunk into the top of the bank. There were gaps in the fencing; some of the uprights leaned drunkenly.

Pete and Anna got out of the truck. Pete took the torch from his pocket and switched it on. 'We'll walk the fence,' he said.

'What do we look for?'

'Disturbed undergrowth, scratch marks, anything.'

They searched for half an hour, while light gradually crept across the sky, fading it from black to grey. The dawn chorus began.

Pete halted and swung the torch around. The beam

probed a clump of bracken. A wide swathe had been trampled through it; broken fronds hung loose. Pete hunkered down and shone his torch across the ditch.

There was a paw print in the earth: four oval pads tipped with long claws: wolf.

'He's here,' Pete said.

They climbed over the fence and entered a copse of oak trees. The ground was soft and springy. There were more wolf tracks, leading to the edge of the copse.

Beyond the trees was open grassland, a road, another copse. Staynor House had been built on the crest of a rise – a Gothic folly, complete with battlements and arrow slits.

Four hundred metres away from Pete and Anna stood a herd of deer. The does were nervous, flicking their scuts; the stag circled them protectively.

'They're spooked,' Pete whispered. 'They know he's watching them, picking out the one that looks weakest.'

'Where is he?'

'I can't tell. Keep watching.'

A shape emerged from the cover of long grass, a hundred and fifty metres to Anna's right: Manitou, moving like a sheepdog working a flock, belly close to the ground, dropping flat whenever a deer looked his way.

'Pete?' said Anna.

'I see him. Let's go for it. Walk easy, and stop when he sees you. Stay upwind so he can get your scent. Call him and try to keep him distracted. I'll come up behind him.'

Anna only took ten paces before Manitou turned his head in her direction; she froze.

'Manitou!' she said.

His ears pricked.

'Manitou!'

He recognised her voice and stood upright. The stag bellowed; the does milled around, keeping close to one another.

'Come on, Manitou!'

Anna held out her clenched fist.

Manitou came in a straight line, eyes fixed on her, gathering speed. When he was fifty metres away he stopped, put back his ears and pranced, ducking his head and whimpering.

'Come on, Manitou!'

Something thudded into Manitou's side, knocking

him off his feet and rolling him over.

There was the sound of a gunshot.

Manitou yelped, a grating squeal that went on and on. He arched his body and snapped at the wound in his flank, fighting the pain as if it were an enemy that could be forced back.

Anna ran forwards howling, 'N-o-o!'

Another thud; another gunshot. Manitou jerked; his paws trembled, then went still.

Anna reached Manitou and fell to her knees, sobbing. He looked smaller. His muzzle was coated with blood and froth. Anna stroked his mane, pushing her fingers through the rough outer coat into the warm teddy-bear fur beneath.

She heard Pete say, 'Anna?'

Anna couldn't speak.

'Anna?'

Words came in a rush. Even though she knew that it was too late, Anna said, 'Help me stop the bleeding, Pete. Call a vet. If we hurry, we can—'

'Anna, he's gone,' Pete said.

Anna went on caressing Manitou's mane. 'He's so beautiful, Pete. Why couldn't he have cubs? If he'd had cubs, it would be like part of him was left.'

Pete said, 'You can't bring him back.'

A man approached cautiously; Anna couldn't tell where he'd come from; he was wearing a camouflage jacket and holding a rifle fitted with a telescopic sight.

'Stand clear of the animal!' the man called out. 'I repeat – stand clear of the animal!'

Anna's lips curled back. 'Stay away from him, you bastard!' she snarled. 'Stay away!'

She launched herself at the man, intending to pull him down and sink her teeth into his throat.

Pete caught her in his arms. 'It won't do any good, Anna,' he said. 'You have to let go.'

Anna wept for her lost love, the time they wouldn't spend together, the understanding that wouldn't be shared.

The man was bewildered. 'What's going on?' he said. 'I thought the wolf was attacking her.'

'He knew her,' said Pete. 'She wasn't in any danger. We were trying to get him back to the sanctuary.'

'I wasn't to know that, was I? I'm the game warden here. The police warned me to be on the lookout for a wolf. When I saw him going for her, I had to make a split-second decision.'

'And you made the wrong one.'

The warden became brusque. 'You realise this is private property, don't you?' he said. 'Have you obtained the owner's permission to be on his land?'

'You've done your job,' said Pete. 'Now please leave us alone.'

The warden turned away and walked towards the house.

Anna said into Pete's shoulder, 'I'm not going to love anyone or anything again. It hurts too much.'

'Don't, Anna.'

'Love always goes wrong.'

'No it doesn't.'

'Like with Manitou.'

'It wasn't your fault.'

'If I'd only—'

Pete held Anna tighter. 'No,' he said. 'There was nothing else you could have done. If the game warden hadn't shot Manitou, some farmer would have.'

Anna's grief was like fear; she didn't know if she could bear it. 'What am I going to do, Pete?' she whispered.

Pete said, 'You're going to be like a wolf. You're going to make it through and carry on.'

*

Two days later Pete buried Manitou in a hole some volunteers had dug between the trees that lined the approach to the sanctuary. Anna forced herself to be there; she helped Pete fill in the hole and pat the soil flat.

When they'd finished, Anna said, 'Are you going to put up a marker?'

Pete shook his head. 'Markers are for human graves. Manitou deserves better than that.'

'D'you think wolves have souls?'

'I don't know. Do people?'

Anna shrugged.

Pete looked down at the flattened earth. 'I think burying him is like giving him back to the wild.'

'He should never have been taken out of it,' Anna said bitterly.

'Maybe not, but wolves need protection, otherwise they're going to be wiped out.'

'Don't all species become extinct sooner or later?'

'Yes.'

'Then what's the point?'

'Zack says that when an animal becomes extinct, the whole planet loses something.'

'You agree with that?'

'Kind of. It's simpler than that for me. I love wolves. I want them to stick around so I can go on loving them.'

Anna's eyes filled up. 'I don't think I'll ever love a person the way I loved Manitou.'

Pete smiled. 'Then you'll have to find another way to love them,' he said.

17

Anna put off going to see Zack for as long as possible. Whenever Gran suggested it, Anna found an excuse that was genuine, but still an excuse. It wasn't that Anna didn't want to see him, but she felt that she was just about managing her grief for Manitou; if she talked to Zack she might lose control of it.

At breakfast on Anna's last day at Gran's, Gran said, 'Anna, you're not going to leave without saying goodbye to Zack, are you?'

'Um, I'm pretty busy with packing and everything.'

'Do you blame him for what happened to Manitou?'

'No.'

'He thinks that's why you haven't visited him.'

'He's wrong!' said Anna. 'Zack's not to blame, it was an accident.'

'It would mean a great deal to him if you told him that face to face. He's finding it hard to forgive himself.'

'There's nothing to forgive. Someone ought to straighten him out.'

'Agreed!' Gran said with a sigh. 'I've tried – but when did Zack ever listen to me?'

'Hasn't Pete had a go?'

'Pete's in an awkward position. Zack's convinced that Pete is trying to spare his feelings. He's cast himself in the role of Pete's protector. He can't accept it when Pete tries to protect him.'

'The old wolf fighting to retain domination of the pack?'

'Old being the operative word. Zack's been deeply shaken. Running the sanctuary gave him a sense of purpose. Now that he's about to lose that purpose, all he can see in the future is a gradual decline into senility. He's become quite morbid.'

'You mean he's wallowing in self-pity?'

'Quite.'

'You going in to the hospital today?'

'I was planning on popping over there some time this morning.'

'I'll tag along,' said Anna. 'Zack doesn't need forgiveness, he needs a boot up the backside.'

Zack's bed was next to the double doors of a men's ward. His ankle was protected by a frame that looked like a small tent under the sheets and blankets. Anna hardly recognised him; his face was pinched and shrunken.

'Hello, Zack,' she said. 'You look terrible.'

'Well that's made my day!' Zack growled. 'You can go now, thanks.'

'No I can't.' Anna pulled a tubular metal chair to the side of the bed and sat down.

'I suppose your grandmother put you up to this,' said Zack. 'Where is she?'

'Making herself scarce.'

'You have an ominous glint in your eye.'

'Too right I do. Gran tells me you're giving in.'

Zack reclined back on his pillows. 'I'm bowing to the inevitable,' he said. 'I should have packed in the sanctuary months ago, handed it on to someone younger. If I had, Manitou would still be alive.'

'You didn't kill him, Zack.'

'Not directly, but I'm the one responsible.'

Tears swelled in Zack's eyes; Anna fought the urge to join in.

'You might not be in charge any more,' she said, 'but there's plenty you can do, Zack.'

'Such as pottering about the place, finding little odd jobs here and there? My handyman days are over.'

'Such as finishing what you started, instead of walking out on it halfway through. The guy who shot Manitou was aiming at a myth. You want Manitou to have died for nothing?'

Zack bristled. 'Of course not!' he snapped.

'Then go on telling people the truth about wolves.'

Zack's eyes softened. 'Strangely enough, I've been considering something along those lines. A lot of memories of Manitou have been coming back to me, particularly the early days. We didn't give each other an inch. It took a long time for me to win his trust.'

'But you did it, and he won yours. Don't just remember, write it down. If adults won't listen to you, tell schoolkids.'

'They won't pay any attention to an old fogey like me,' Zack said dismissively.

'They will if your story's good enough.'

Zack said quietly, 'Once upon a time there was an

old man who hated being old. To help him forget, he took a young wolf and shut him in a pen. The old man went into the pen and stared at the wolf, and the wolf stared at him, and they were both afraid…'

'Not bad,' said Anna. 'Don't forget the most important part.'

'What's that?'

'How the fear turned into respect and love.'

Zack laughed. 'You are the most exasperating young woman it's ever been my misfortune to meet! You have no intention of allowing me to grow old gracefully, have you?'

'Growing old disgracefully sounds more fun. Here.' Anna placed the book she'd been writing in on Zack's bedside cupboard. 'You can use that. I'm sorry some of the pages are missing. I tore them out.'

Zack picked up the book and riffled the edge of the pages with his thumb. 'You expect me to fill this?' he said.

'Uh-huh.'

'But you're leaving tomorrow. How do you know I'll stick at it when you're not here to browbeat me?'

'My spies will keep me informed.'

Zack sighed. 'I know when I should submit. I'll

stop being a man of action and become a man of letters – satisfied?'

'Almost. Promise me you'll send me what you've written when it's finished.'

'What for?'

'So I can read it. If it's rubbish, I'll tell you and you'll have to do it over again.'

Zack shook his head in admiration. 'I shall miss you, Anna.'

'You'll be too busy.'

'No I shan't. I'm very fond of you, you know. So is Pete – perhaps more than he realises.'

Anna wagged a finger at Zack. 'Knock off the matchmaking, will you? Pete and I are doing OK. You leave us alone, we'll leave you and Gran alone – deal?'

'Deal,' said Zack.

On the road out of town, Gran said, 'You pulled Zack up by his bootstraps. That's the most on form he's been since the accident.'

'I told him you wouldn't marry him unless he cheered up,' said Anna.

Gran pursed her lips. 'I'll ignore that cheap remark.

What made you suggest that he should write about his experiences?'

'Instinct.'

'It was inspired. Zack has a flair for writing, though he's neglected it since his wife died. It'll be good therapy for him.'

'Like staying with you has been good therapy for me. I don't want to go home tomorrow, Gran. I'm dreading it.'

'After what you've been through this summer, it shouldn't be difficult.'

'But I'm not the same. I can't be the person I was before.'

'Be yourself.'

'I don't know if Mum and Dad and my friends will be able to handle it.'

'They'll come around. Have more faith in yourself.'

'I'll try,' said Anna. 'So what's going to happen with you and Zack?'

'That's our affair,' Gran said primly. 'But if Alzheimer's sets in and I accept his next proposal, we'll send you an invitation to the wedding.'

'You're going to say yes next time?'

Gran smiled. 'Wouldn't you like to know,' she said.

'Thanks, Gran.'

'For?'

'Everything.'

'That's what grandmothers are for.'

'No it's not. I've learned so much from you.'

'You've learned from yourself,' said Gran. 'I'm not taking any of the credit. Oh, and while we're on the subject of your return home, I hope you don't mind but I won't be coming with you to the station. I loathe prolonged goodbyes. Pete's offered to run you to the station.'

Anna giggled. 'You never let up, do you, Gran?'

'No,' said Gran, 'and neither do you. It's in the genes. Use it wisely.'

Anna and Pete stood on the platform, waiting for the eleven fifteen. Anna noticed a photo booth, remembered Matt and smiled.

'Will you stay in touch?' said Pete.

'Yes, phone calls, letters. Are you on-line?'

'Not yet. Am I going to see you again?'

'You bet! I'll be down for weekends whenever I can. It's half term at the end of October. My folks think they're taking me to Italy, but they've got another think coming.'

'It won't be the same without you around.'

'Good.'

The station announcer said, 'The next train to arrive at Platform Five will be the eleven fifteen to—'

Pete and Anna went into a hug.

Pete said, 'Don't forget about me.'

'I'm not going to.'

The train drew up; doors opened and passengers spilled out.

Anna and Pete drew apart.

'Please don't watch me go,' said Anna. 'You'll make me cry.'

Pete held Anna's face in his hands, leaned down and kissed her gently on the lips. 'Take care of yourself,' he said.

Anna boarded the train and found a seat; she looked out of the window, but Pete had already gone.

She thought: The next time I see him, we'll be saying hello.

Anna held on to the thought as the train pulled out of the station.

Black Apples from Orchard Books

☐ If Only I'd Known	Jenny Davis	1 84121 789 1	£4.99
☐ Bitter Fruit	Brian Keaney	1 84121 005 6	£4.99
☐ Balloon House	Brian Keaney	1 84121 437 X	£4.99
☐ Family Secrets	Brian Keaney	1 84121 530 9	£4.99
☐ The Private Life of Georgia Brown	Brian Keaney	1 84121 528 7	£4.99
☐ Get a Life	Jean Ure	1 84121 831 6	£4.99
☐ Just Sixteen	Jean Ure	1 84121453 1	£4.99

Orchard Black Apples are available from all good bookshops, or can be
ordered direct from the publisher:
Orchard Books, PO BOX 29, Douglas IM99 1BQ
Credit card orders please telephone 01624 836000
or fax 01624 837033 or visit our Internet site: www.wattspub.co.uk
or e-mail: bookshop@enterprise.net for details.

To order please quote title, author and ISBN
and your full name and address.
Cheques and postal orders should be made payable to
'Bookpost plc.'
Postage and packing is FREE within the UK
(overseas customers should add £1.00 per book).
Prices and availability are subject to change